CATCH THE COUGAR

A HALLOWEEN NOVELLA

TERRY SPEAR

PUBLISHED BY:
Terry Spear

Catch the Cougar
Copyright © 2020 by Terry Spear
Cover by Terry Spear

All rights reserved. No part of this book may be reproduced or transmitted in any form or by any means, electronic or mechanical, including photocopying, recording, or by any information storage and retrieval system, without written permission from the author, except for the inclusion of brief quotations in a review.

Discover more about Terry Spear at:
http://www.terryspear.com
ISBN Print: 978-1-63311-063-2
ISBN E-Book: 978-1-63311-062-5

To Gail Dockery who needs a Halloween cougar fix. Thanks so much for loving my shifters!

SYNOPSIS

Cougar shifter Vanessa Vanderbilt is Yuma Town's veterinarian, and though she's attracted to sexy William Rugel, family physician, he's on her least favorite list of doctors in town. After all, why wouldn't he be when he thinks veterinarians aren't smart enough to make it in medical school? Top that off with the issue of her being stood up twice at the altar, and by different grooms, no less!—so taking up with another cougar *isn't* in the plans.

William Rugel has no idea why Vanessa, who he is extremely attracted to, won't give him the time of day. But everyone in Yuma Town is determined to get the two of them together and he'll do whatever it takes to prove to her he's one of the good guys. Even take in a puppy because he knows she adores animals. So does he, but he hadn't planned to get a dog to get a date!

It's time for another cougar Halloween party—and since Vanessa had met her last two fiancés at Halloween parties, who knows what will come of this one!

CHAPTER 1

Vanessa Vanderbilt, Doctor of Veterinary Medicine, loved working in Yuma Town, totally cougar run, and she had enough business to keep her busy with just the cougars' pets: dogs, horses, and cats, and the occasional cougar that dropped in to have an injury taken care of when in their cougar form. Sometimes, she even helped with cougars in labor who were having multiple births. Her favorite physician to work with at times like that was Kate Parker Hill. Which meant Dr. William Rugel was her least favorite doctor to work with. If only his striking good looks, his nearly black hair and green eyes, quirky smiles, cute little frowns, and disarming expressions could mean anything to her. Sometimes she would run into him when he was wearing a little bit of a five o'clock shadow that really turned her on, *if* he wasn't her least favorite doctor to work with.

At least for now. She'd heard how he thought veterinarians were doctors who weren't smart enough to be physicians for human patients. What did he know?

She had to be the jack of all trades when it came to the numerous kinds of animals that she had to take care of. Including cougars. She'd also been happier around animals than she had been around humans anyway, while growing up.

Shannon Buchanan brought in the family's black Newfoundland, Muddy, for vaccine shots and Vanessa smiled at him as she checked him over. "He's looking good. Good weight, coat looks great, teeth are perfect. You're doing a great job. What about Sassy and Shadow?" The ginger cats were adorable.

"I have another appointment tomorrow. I couldn't manage all three of them on my own today. Chase is taking the girls in for their vaccinations as we speak. So what are you doing for Halloween this year?"

"I don't usually go to those things." Vanessa preferred staying at home out a way from Yuma Town where her vet practice was. She was on-call all the time, though she didn't get called after hours too often. Her wildest case since she'd moved here was capturing skunks at Geoffrey and Grace Robinson's house, while their niece, Nina, had been hiding out there. It was just one of those very interesting cases, topped with a skunk issue.

"You've got to come. We have so much fun," Shannon persisted.

"I guess I could come as a vet wearing a lab coat."

Shannon tsked. "You have to wear a costume. That's the fun of it."

"I'll think on it."

"We'll have a pumpkin-carving contest, bobbing for apples, food, drinks, hayrides, pony rides for the kids, and then a dance."

"I'll probably be at home watching *Hocus Pocus* or *Sleepy Hollow*."

"Aha! So you do like Halloween. Besides"—Shannon motioned to all the fall and Halloween decorations: fall leaf garlands, pumpkins, jack-o'-lanterns, black cats, including a real one sleeping behind the counter that was Vanessa's Midnight —"you have decorated all out this year."

"It makes my clients happy." Vanessa finished up the vaccinations for Muddy, then gave him a cheese treat. It made her happy too, but she didn't want to admit it. "These shots are good for three years."

"Oh, good. All right. Well, we'll be disappointed if you don't come to the party."

"I'll think on it."

"Okay, I hope you change your mind. You would have fun. See you later." Shannon left the clinic with Muddy.

Vanessa really did keep busy with taking care of animals, so when she had time off, she liked to chill. She was lousy at pumpkin carving, and bobbing for apples, no way. Dancing? She wouldn't have a dance partner. She sighed. What would she even wear anyway?

Her cougar fur coat? She smiled.

~

Dr. William Rugel greeted Chase Buchanan as he brought in the girls for their immunizations. "Shannon gave you the job this time." Chase owned the resort out on Lake Buchanan and was a part-time deputy sheriff for Yuma Town. He and Shannon had been great at welcoming William to the community. Though so did everyone else. He loved the cougar-run town, compared to when he was working at a human hospital.

Chase smiled. "She took Muddy in for his vaccination instead."

"Oh, okay. So the whole family is having them done."

"Yeah, the cats are scheduled for tomorrow. Shannon's and my immunizations are up to date. You're coming to the Halloween party, aren't you, Doc?"

The girls both said, "You have to!"

William smiled. "I wouldn't miss it for the world." Doc

finished up the kids' shots and he gave them each a colorful, plastic ring from a treasure box.

"Good. What will you be?" Chase asked.

"A warrior. A Highlander, maybe. Or a high-fantasy fighter. I'm not sure."

"A pirate!" Sadie said.

"Yeah, a pirate!" Zoey, her six-year-old twin sister said, agreeing with her.

William smiled. "I'll have to see what is in my magic chest of costumes."

"That sounds good. Well, I've got to get the kids home. Talk to you later, Doc."

"See you soon." William was thinking he needed to ask someone to go with him to the party since there would be dancing. Then again, maybe he would just meet someone there and ask her to dance. After the failed relationship he'd had at the last hospital he worked at, he didn't want to go through that turmoil again anytime soon.

Now if only he did have a magic chest of costumes, he would be all set. He'd forgotten all about the Halloween party. He was glad Chase had mentioned it to him.

Dr. Kate Parker Hill, who had convinced him to join her at the clinic, peeked into his office while he was catching up on patient records. "Did I hear you say you're going to the Halloween party?"

He smiled. "I wouldn't miss it for the world." He just needed a date.

CHAPTER 2

It was finally time to call it a day when Vanessa carried Midnight to their home, situated behind the vet clinic so she could go in if she needed to in a hurry for an emergency. It was chilly, the fall colors beautiful in oranges and reds and purples. Evergreens filled the landscape too.

She saw a hitchhiker wearing a dark gray hoody, slouched in the chilly breeze, trying to keep warm, gray jeans and sneakers and no one she knew, walking along the road. It would take him about half an hour walking to the businesses in town and she hoped he would make it just fine. She smiled at the beautiful decorations she had for Halloween outside: scarecrows, jack-o'-lanterns, black cats, and pumpkins. Yeah, she loved to decorate for fall and Halloween. And as a kid, she loved to trick-or-treat. In college, she always enjoyed attending Halloween parties. Once she became a vet in Yuma Town, there hadn't seemed to be as much time for it. Not to mention when she had lived in Colorado Springs, she'd met both of her former fiancés at Halloween parties two separate years. Which had kind of soured Halloween parties for her.

She sighed. She ought to check Yuma Town's out. At least here, she would be among cougars and friends

She walked inside her home, smelled the aroma of beef stew that made her stomach rumble and she couldn't wait to eat. She released Midnight to eat her own food and locked the door. Vanessa figured her hearty beef stew cooking in the slow cooker would be ready to eat by now. She was about to serve it up when someone knocked on her door.

She answered the door and was surprised to see the hooded hitchhiker. "Yes?"

He was shivering, and he appeared to be suffering from the mild effects of hypothermia.

"I...my car broke down."

"Did you call for a tow service?"

"My...my phone battery died."

"Come in, you can get warmed up, and you can call from here." She let him into the house and motioned to her house phone.

But he didn't make a move toward it. Maybe he was more hypothermic than she originally thought. "I'll get you something hot to drink. Coffee?"

"Yeah, thanks." He was still shivering hard, his blue eyes glancing around her place.

She went into the kitchen that was open to the living room and started the coffee. "I'll call a tow service for you." She wanted to get him help so he would be taken care of and out of here, and she would have dinner, curl up with Midnight on the couch, watch a movie, and relax.

"Put the phone down," he said, this time sounding more himself. His eyes began to water, and he sneezed.

She set the phone on its cradle. Okay, letting him into the house had been a big mistake. She wished she could turn into her cougar and show him he couldn't mess with her and get away with it.

The phone suddenly rung, making her jump. She saw it was Dan Steinacker, their sheriff on the caller ID. She glanced at the man in her home. "My new boyfriend. He'll be over here checking on me if I don't answer the phone."

"Don't say anything you shouldn't."

Right. She answered the phone. "Hi, Dan, about our date tonight, I think we'll need to postpone it. I've got a lot of paperwork to do."

Dan was dead silent, and she knew he realized she was in trouble, thankfully.

"Yeah, honey, we can do that. I've got some student tests I need to grade, so maybe tomorrow night?" Dan asked, even though he'd never taught class in his life, and he was a mated cougar.

"Yeah, that would be great."

"All right, well, I'm going to scrounge up some dinner. Night, see you tomorrow then."

"Night, Dan." She suspected he and his deputies were already trying to locate this man and had called to warn her about him being in her area—too late for that.

"Okay, what do you want?" she asked the man.

"Keys to your car. And you're coming with me."

Giving him the keys to her car was fine, well, not fine, but she could always replace the car. No way did she want to go with him. He pulled out a gun, shocking her. Okay, so he wasn't bluffing about being in charge. She wondered why he hadn't already pulled out his gun, but then she realized he must have been so hypothermic he wasn't thinking clearly. She was afraid if she said no to going with him, he'd shoot her right there and then take her car anyway. But going with him wasn't a much better option. He could kill her anywhere along the road and dump her body.

She wished she had her tranquilizer gun within reach that she used to tranquilize wild animals needing her care. Only this time the wild animal would go straight to jail, then be hauled off to Loveland. They didn't keep humans long term in their Yuma Town jail.

"I need to change into something warmer." She headed for her bedroom, hoping he would go along with the plan.

"Wait."

She thought if only she could reach her room, she could lock her door, open her window, strip, shift and leap out the window. But she couldn't have him see her shift or she'd have to turn him or kill him. No way would they want a criminal to become one of their kind. She just needed to stall for time.

Then she heard car engines draw closer to her home and shut off. The cavalry was parking way out so they didn't tip their hand. The human couldn't hear them like she could.

He stood in her bedroom doorway while she pulled a warm, wool shirt and sweater out of her drawer. She unbuttoned her blouse. With her sensitive cat hearing, she heard people moving around outside the house. Good news!

But then she worried this guy would use her as a shield when Dan and his men tried to arrest him.

"Hurry it up. We don't have all day," the man snapped and then he sneezed again. He frowned. "Do you have a cat?"

Luckily, Midnight had made herself scarce, as if she sensed this man was dangerous.

Vanessa shook her head. She was afraid he would hurt Midnight if he learned she was here, and it appeared he was highly allergic to cats. His nose was running, and his eyes were blurry with tears. Good one on him.

She wasn't even sure why he was letting her get changed out

of her clothes though, but it could work to her advantage. She pulled off her pumps and brought out her hiking boots and a pair of jeans as if she was going on a forest hike. Then she removed her trousers and socks. All she was wearing now was her bra and panties.

Yank them off and shift, her cougar voice was telling her. Take him down before he knows what even hit him.

But her human voice told her the sheriff and his deputies were here and she needed to let them do their job. Not to mention, the man still had a gun.

She was a cougar though, damn it, and as long as Midnight stayed hidden, probably under her bed, Vanessa was going to do something about this. She wasn't going to let the man take her hostage in front of the sheriff, which could have a bad outcome no matter how she looked at it. She unfastened her bra and tossed it onto the bed.

"What the hell are you doing?" the man asked, looking shocked.

"I need to put warmer clothes on." Warmer as in her natural cougar fur coat. She tugged off her panties.

Someone knocked on the front door. The man turned to look. She shifted and lunged.

~

William had gotten the call from Dan, telling him Vanessa might be hurt if the two-time, convicted armed robber—who had escaped from the jail at Loveland, Colorado—injured her. William was on standby near where all the sheriff and deputies' vehicles were parked, per Dan's strict orders. He hadn't wanted the doctor injured if things went south.

In the worst way, William wanted to shift into his cougar and take out the man himself if he so much as threatened Vanessa. She was an appealing blond with blue eyes that always seem to see clear through to William's soul, though she never gave him the time of day and he wasn't sure what he'd done to irk her. There was no figuring women. But he sure wanted to make things better between them. Sure, she was civil with him, but her whole posture said that was as far as she would take it with him.

He wanted more. If he rescued her, maybe she would see him differently.

He heard snarling in the house. *Great.* She'd shifted. He hadn't expected that. He hadn't thought she would be that unpredictable.

She was a loaded pistol ready to go off—if William's guess as to what was going on inside her home was any indication. He ran toward the house as Dan and his deputies—Stryker Hill, Chase Buchanan, and Hal Haverton—hurried inside. He didn't have a gun, so he wasn't sure what he thought he would do! But he couldn't sit back in the wings and wait if Vanessa was in trouble.

William raced inside to see Vanessa as a golden cougar, sitting on top of the convict's back, his eyes shut and she was growling low as if the man was her prey and she wasn't giving him up to anyone.

"We've got this," Dan said, his gun out, ready to shoot the robber if he as much as moved to hurt Vanessa.

She glanced at William, her eyes narrowed, and he held his hands up in his defense. "I'm only here at Dan's request in case you were injured."

She got off the man and disappeared down the hall.

Chase was handcuffing the convict while Stryker was reading him his rights. Then they hauled the man out of her house while Dan and Hal stayed behind to get Vanessa's statement.

William felt she didn't need him, but he was staying there just to make sure.

When she returned to the living room wearing jeans and a

sweater and little pink, fluffy slippers, he had to smile. She didn't though. She looked furious.

"Are you all right?" William asked.

"Yes. Thanks. You can go now."

"Good." He knew when he wasn't wanted. A lot of she-cats found him appealing. He had no idea why Vanessa didn't. He headed out the door, glad she wasn't hurt at least and that they'd arrested the convict. So much for saving her and changing her mind about him.

~

"What was the man wanted for?" Vanessa asked Dan as Midnight came out and greeted them, and the guys petted and cuddled her.

"The man just robbed a store in Loveland and crashed a stolen car near here. Then we learned he was an escaped felon from the Loveland jail, and we organized a search party. We were all trying to locate him and started to put the town on alert that he would be on foot close by where he left the car and not to open the door to anyone. But when I called you to warn you—based on your response—I knew you were in trouble."

"I saw him hitchhiking on the road headed for town. He looked like he wasn't wearing enough clothes to keep himself warm so when he came to my door, I couldn't let him die of hypothermia. Even so, it was a mistake to answer the door and let him in." She sat down on her couch and Midnight jumped on her lap and curled up, purring and watching Dan and Hal—everything right with her world again.

"You were able to shift out of his sight?" Dan asked, frowning.

"I removed my clothes in front of him. That's all he saw."

Smiling, Hal shook his head.

"Remind me not to piss you off," Dan said.

She rolled her eyes. "I was trying to stall him from stealing my car, taking me hostage, and driving me somewhere else. That was his plan. Anyway, then one of you guys knocked on the door and that made him turn his head. And I shifted and took him down. So he never saw me shift."

"That's what we had to know," Dan said. "Are you going to be all right by yourself?"

"Yeah, thanks, Dan. I'm fine. I'm just going to grab some beef stew and watch something lighthearted on TV."

"If you need anyone, just let us know," Hal said. "Sometimes after an incident like this, you can feel...unnerved."

Now would be the time to have a boyfriend. Real, not pretend. But she was really too busy for that. She was glad to move to Yuma Town where there were so many cougars willing to help each other in a pinch. She wasn't one to ask, but it was nice knowing she could. Take this situation. She'd never lived anywhere that she could talk to the sheriff during a crisis and he would know right away that she was in trouble and he would call up the troops.

They seemed reluctant to leave her alone though, which she thought was sweet.

"Are you sure you don't want to come out to the ranch and stay with Tracey and me?" Hal asked. "We have plenty of room and you might feel a bit more secure."

"Or you can stay with Addie and me," Dan said. "When you've had trouble like this, you can feel unsettled."

"I'll be fine. Thanks for the offers though. You caught the escaped convict and I'm good. Thanks, guys."

Dan and Hal hesitantly left, after they wished her a good night, and she did feel a little bad that she'd dismissed William like she had. But she was still sore about how he thought a medical doctor had to be smarter than a veterinarian. She was proud of what she did and wouldn't have wanted to be a medical practitioner and take care of human patients. Though here, they were cougars, but when she first got her license to practice, she didn't even know about Yuma Town.

She turned on a light comedy on TV about an undercover bodyguard serving as a bridesmaid at a wedding when she detested weddings, all due to being jilted at the alter by her fiancé.

Vanessa scoffed and served up her hearty beef stew, then carried her tray to the couch. Try *two* weddings where she'd been stood up and the protagonist could hate weddings and definitely not trust suitors to follow through. Not that anyone in Yuma Town knew that about her. She didn't want *anyone* to know it. The pain from two groom no-shows at her weddings had still been raw after she first had moved to Yuma Town. What did that say about her? That she couldn't keep a man?

She snorted.

~

At his townhouse, William grabbed a package of the last two slices of sharp cheddar cheese to make a grilled cheese sandwich before they went bad and frowned at the green mold growing on it. Skip that. He put away the bread and threw out the cheese. He knew he should have eaten it sooner. He pulled out frozen burritos, heated them, grabbed a beer, and settled down on the couch to watch a thriller on TV, but—despite the riveting action as the protagonist chased the villain's henchman on motorcycles through the streets of Paris—he couldn't stop thinking about Vanessa and the way she had been sitting as a cougar on top of the armed, escaped convict in her home.

He grabbed his phone to call her and make sure she was okay but then thought better of it. He set his phone on the console. He watched more of the show, then sighed and picked up his phone again. It rang in his hand and he almost dropped it. He glanced at the caller ID and smiled. Vanessa...DVM.

"Hello?" He quickly paused the movie. "Are you okay?"

"Yeah, sorry I was so short with you. I...shouldn't have been."

"After going through what you did, it was understandable. Any of us could have felt that way."

"Yeah, but I only reacted that way to you. I'm sorry."

"Apology excepted. Hey, did you want to have dinner with me tomorrow night?"

"Uh, no, thanks for the offer. Well, I'm going to go. Good night."

"Thanks for calling, and I'm glad you are okay. Good night."

"Thanks." Then she ended the call.

He sat there staring at the phone. Then he smiled. She had finally talked to him. He didn't know why he was so hung up on her. He never had trouble with making friends with women, though sometimes his hours were long and that cut into his dating time. But for some reason, he just wanted to get to know her. Maybe because she was as dedicated to her work as he was. Maybe because she went out of her way to avoid him. And that made her a challenge.

He really wanted to be friends with her. Not that it would lead to courting or anything, though that certainly was something he was willing to explore. But he just hated that she didn't even seem to *want* to be friends. He wondered—as he started his movie again—if she thought he was a womanizer. He wasn't. He really hadn't dated anyone here. He was just...friendly. He wondered if she took that as him not being able to commit to a relationship. The only reason he hadn't yet was that no one had interested him enough to make a commitment here in Yuma Town.

Would Vanessa? Maybe not, but he loved the way she smiled when others were visiting with her at cougar activities—not at him though, and he wanted to change that—how she talked so animatedly with her hands, how, it didn't matter where she was, she would address pet issues with her clients. Heck, at a party, *he* wouldn't discuss medical issues with his own patients! He would tell his patients it all had to do with privacy issues. Of course that was some of it, but when he was off from work, he wanted to be *off*.

His cell rang again and he thought he got lucky and Vanessa had changed her mind about going out with him for dinner tomorrow night, but it was Kate, and that probably meant he had to go in about an emergency.

"I heard about tonight." Kate didn't say anything further.

He sighed. "Yeah, Kate?" He wasn't going to volunteer anything and feel foolish because he said too much.

"Hal said that Vanessa dismissed you when you were there in case that convict had injured her."

"Uh, yeah, well, you know, she was under a lot of strain. She called and apologized."

"Oh." Kate sounded immensely relieved. "Good, I'm so glad to hear it. So what are you going to do about it?"

"About what, exactly?" Again, he wasn't second-guessing Kate. She had said any number of times that he should ask Vanessa out, but he'd done that now, and it was still a no-go.

"Asking her out?"

He let out his breath in a heavy sigh. "I asked her when she said she was sorry, and she said no."

"Oh. Well, keep trying. Everyone in the cougar community loves you."

"Except for Vanessa." William paused the movie.

"So what's the deal with that? We kept thinking that things would change between the two of you."

He scoffed. "I haven't the faintest idea. Maybe she thinks I'm too flirtatious with other women or something."

"But you aren't. You know, she's really secretive about her past."

Now that revelation made William curious. "I figured you ladies would know all about her because of your little shopping trips and get-togethers."

"Nope. All we know is she came through here on a trip up north and realized we were cougar run, we didn't have a vet clinic, and she wanted to start one. We were thrilled of course."

"You haven't ever talked to her about dating?"

"No. And if we had, we wouldn't share that with anyone."

He sighed. "Okay, thanks, Kate, and we're good."

Kate didn't say anything, and he knew what she was thinking. Vanessa still didn't care for him for whatever reason, and yet, the oddest thing was, he sometimes caught her looking at him, as if she was interested in him—not as though she couldn't stand the sight of him. He sighed. Women. There was no figuring them.

"Good night, Kate."

"Night, William. See you tomorrow at the clinic."

He set his phone down on the console and restarted his movie. How was he going to learn more about Vanessa's past if she wouldn't speak with him?

Then the phone rang again. He was popular tonight. He checked the phone and saw it was Vanessa. He frowned and said, "Hey, is anything wrong?" Maybe she was calling to tell him she was having dinner with him after all.

"You think veterinarians aren't as smart as family physicians or they would have been able to go to medical school."

His jaw dropped. Hell, when had he said that? He'd always joked with a childhood friend—who had become a vet—about that, but William had only been having some fun. And Matt had always told William right back that he didn't have to know how to take care of tons of different species of animals. Which William agreed with. He couldn't remember a time when he had been talking to his friend about it where she would have overheard him.

"Uh—"

"So you do." She sounded annoyed with him.

He had to rectify this situation in a hurry, if that was all that was keeping her from being friends with him. "When did you hear me say that? I was talking to a friend from my youth who became a vet. We kidded each other all the time about it. But he always told me he was so much smarter than me because he had to deal with so many different kinds of animals."

"What?"

"When did you hear me talking to my friend about it?"

"When the town celebrated my arrival and the opening of my vet clinic. You were having a beer and talking with Leyton when you got a call. You weren't very far away from me when you made the comment, though with our cougar hearing, I could have heard you even if I had been further away."

"Well, Vanessa, I'm so sorry. I was just joking with my friend. He'd called while I was at the party and I was telling him we had our first vet who had just opened her clinic and that's when we got into the same old thing we always did—me being smarter than him, him being smarter than me. He's human or I would have told him he should set up a practice here."

She sighed. "Where are you taking me for dinner tomorrow night?"

He smiled. "Anywhere you would like."

"Your place, grilled barbecue chicken, hamburgers, steak, whatever you're good at."

"Tomorrow night." Hell, William didn't have a grill. He was always working or going to Hal's, Leyton's, Chase's, Dan's, Jack's, or Stryker's place for barbecue. He always got invited and he always went.

"Yeah. Is that okay? Around six-thirty?"

"Yeah, sure. That would be great." He looked at his messy townhouse: clothes strewn all about, pots and pans in the sink. At least he put his dishes in the dishwasher. "I can't wait to see you then."

"I'm sorry for thinking the worst of you."

"No problem. I'm just glad we cleared the air." He had to call Leyton pronto and work down the list to see who could loan him a grill that wouldn't be too much trouble to haul over to his back patio, if Leyton couldn't loan his. William smiled. He was finally going to have a date with Vanessa.

"Okay, me too. I'll see you tomorrow." She ended the call.

He wished his nurse friend, Marcus Jones, who lived in the townhouse adjoining his, had a grill, but his stopped working a month ago and he hadn't replaced it. William called Leyton first. "Hey, uhm, I've got a date with Vanessa for tomorrow night, but she wants me to barbecue."

"That's great. I'm so glad to hear it."

"I don't have a grill."

CHAPTER 3

Vanessa sighed and went to bed. She felt bad that she had thought the worst of William when he had just been joking with his friend. Though the part of his conversation that she had overheard had sounded bad. Having dinner with William didn't mean anything more would come of it, but it was the least she could do since he'd already asked her, and she wanted to make amends.

She hoped he was fine with barbecuing their meal. She should have let him choose what he wanted to do rather than request that, if he wanted to order takeout or something. She wasn't picky about food and she figured he might be as tired as she was after a long day in the clinic. She thought of calling him back, but she didn't. It was time to sleep, work tomorrow, and then have dinner with William, and she was looking forward to it.

If things worked out well at dinner that night, she could have him over for dinner sometime at her place, but she didn't want to tell anyone else in Yuma Town about it. Her long-term relationships had led to an almost-marriage both times, and she didn't want anyone to even speculate that having dinner once or twice with William meant they were headed in that direction. As close-knit as the cougar family was, she could just imagine everyone suddenly inviting them to their homes as if they were a couple already, hoping to ensure the fantasy became a reality—as if pretending it was so, made it so.

After two grooms had stood her up at the altar, she certainly wasn't looking for that kind of relationship again. Then again, what if she and William had nothing to talk about, nothing in common, and the dinner conversation was a total fizzle? Anything was possible.

She closed her eyes and felt Midnight jump on the bed and curl up between her legs. And that made Vanessa wonder if William even liked cats. Or pets in general. She knew he didn't have one.

She rolled onto her side, forcing Midnight to move and she curled up next to Vanessa's waist. Midnight was a rescue cat, at a time when Vanessa was through with men and Midnight had been a welcome addition to her little family.

Vanessa sighed. She was way overthinking this business with William and if she didn't get some sleep, she would be worthless at the clinic in the morning and even worse by tomorrow night when she went over to have dinner with him.

Kate entered William's office at the clinic early the next morning, and said, "Okay, Leyton dropped off his grill this morning at your townhouse before he had to run off to chase down a renegade cougar down south." Leyton, Kate's mate, was an agent with the Cougar Special Forces, and he was always having to run off after some rogue cougar or another.

"Tell him thanks so much."

"What else can we do to help?"

"I've got it under control. I just didn't have the grill."

Kate frowned at him and folded her arms. "What made her change her mind about you?"

William told her about the party celebrating her joining them in Yuma Town and what he'd said to his vet friend.

Kate laughed. "Oh, if that is all."

"That's enough. I mean, if the roles had been reversed, and I didn't know she was talking to a friend of hers in jest, I might have taken offense, figuring she didn't see my worth as a vet. So I understand how she felt."

"Okay, it's a relief that you two are finally socializing and she's not going to be glowering at you whenever she sees you. Oh, and by the way, if you really want to get on her good side, she adores animals, so get a pet. That's why she's a vet. She's kind of a wallflower when it comes to large gatherings. But put her in a room full of pets and she's in her element." Kate patted him on the shoulder. "And don't let this one go."

William smiled. Getting a pet wasn't something he had in mind to do and he had no idea if he and Vanessa would even like each other enough to date. They were only having dinner, at least for now. Maybe he would be able to get to know her a little better and things between them would really change.

~

"We've got a mission," Bridget MacKay told Addie Steinacker, a deputy sheriff on maternity leave from the deputy sheriff's office in Yuma Town, who was mated to Dan, the sheriff. Once Kate had called Bridget to see if she could do some undercover work while she was on maternity leave also, except she was with the Cougar Special Forces, or CSF, as a special agent, Bridget knew she and Addie had to do the job together. Bridget's mate, Travis, was also CSF and she was sure he would frown on what she and Addie were about to embark on

—a mission to learn about Vanessa Vanderbilt's romantic relationships in Colorado Springs, Colorado, where she had come from. Addie's mate would probably tell them both to butt out too.

Addie and Dan's gray and white striped tabby cat had to go to the vet for her annual checkup this morning and Bridget thought they could use that excuse to get some intel on Vanessa during the vet visit. This would be a strictly clandestine operation that only she and Addie and Kate would know about.

"Oh, good. I'm so ready to take a break and do something investigative. So what are we checking out?" Addie sounded as thrilled about the prospect as Bridget felt.

Bridget cleared her throat. "We're looking into Vanessa's former love life."

There was a significant pause.

"What?" Addie finally said.

"Okay, Kate said that William and Vanessa are having their first dinner tonight. We need to learn what her dating history was before this so we can advise William on how to handle himself."

Addie laughed.

"I'm serious. You know how much he has wanted to be friends with her since she arrived, and she has pushed him away at every chance they had at socializing. But things have changed between them and he really wants to make this work."

"William told you that?"

"Oh, no, Kate did. Apparently, Vanessa wanted William to grill her dinner and he doesn't have a grill even! So he asked Kate, and Leyton checked around to see who could help him haul his grill over to William's townhouse so William would be all set."

Addie laughed again. "Does Vanessa know that all of cougar town will be conspiring to make this happen?"

"Hopefully not. That's why we need to do this in a really subtle way."

"Okay, what about doing an investigation into William's romantic liaisons? I mean, this should go both ways," Addie said.

"You're right. Absolutely. We'll investigate William too, and then we can let Vanessa know if he's a good fit for her."

"You know we could let them figure this out on their own, just like I did with Dan and you did with Travis."

Bridget thought about it for a moment. "Nah, we need a case to work on, and this is really important. Not once have either of them dated anyone else since they have been in Yuma Town, yet both of them are interested in each other."

"And you know this how?" Addie asked.

"At every function we've had, they search each other out in a surreptitious way. We all notice it though. You know how it is with us being curious cats."

"And? Ohmigod, you've read their minds, right?" Addie chuckled. "And you'll be using your mind-spy powers to read their thoughts when you question them, I bet."

"Yeah. He's been dying to enjoy her company, and she can't keep her eyes off him, admiring him, but being annoyed with him too. It's like this real contradiction where her feelings toward him are concerned. If we can help them out, don't you want to give it a try?"

"Sure."

"Good. I'll go with you to take in your cat and we can ask some questions of her that seem innocuous and it won't have anything to do with her dating William at all."

"Okay, I'm game. I'm leaving at nine and I'll pick you up at your house."

"Good, see you in half an hour then."

∽

*V*anessa finished up another annual pet exam and gave the dog its vaccinations when Addie Steinacker showed up with her cat for her physical. Vanessa was surprised to see Bridget MacKay had come with her. She guessed the two women were ready to take a break from motherhood.

"How is Lucy doing?" Vanessa asked Addie.

"Oh, just fine."

"She looks nice and healthy. Teeth look good. Heartbeat sounds fine. I'll do some bloodwork on her, to check for heartworms."

Addie glanced at Bridget, who just smiled, then said, "So when you were living in Colorado Springs, you worked at a vet clinic that was human run, didn't you?"

"Uh, yes. I'll just take Lucy back into the other room and be out in a minute."

Vanessa and her vet technician, Riley Manning, whom she had hired recently to help out at the clinic, took Lucy to another room in the back.

∽

*A*ddie frowned at Bridget. "You were supposed to start questioning her," she whispered.

"I had every intention of doing so, but I realized it was kind of awkward when she's talking to you about Lucy, which is why we are here."

Addie pursed her lips. "Okay, invite her over to dinner. Travis went out of town with Leyton to chase after bad guys, you're going to be alone, and so is Kate. You could say you're going to get together with Kate, and did she want to come too?"

"What if she did and she canceled on poor William?"

Vanessa returned with the cat and Riley.

Both Addie and Bridget smiled at Vanessa.

"She looks good. And she's all set for another year," Vanessa said.

"Oh, good," Addie said, taking her cat into her arms. "Thanks so much."

"You're welcome."

As they were leaving to pay at the reception counter, Bridget said to Addie, loud enough for Vanessa to hear, "We've got to get Tracey's sister, Jessie, married off."

Addie frowned at her, then as if she realized it was another of Bridget's ploys to read a person's mind when they reacted to something they saw or heard, she nodded. "Oh, yes. Soon."

Then Addie paid the vet bill and they headed out to the car with Lucy in her carrier.

"So?" Addie asked, climbing into the vehicle.

"Vanessa began thinking of a movie she was watching last night about an undercover bodyguard serving as a bridesmaid at a wedding."

Addie laughed. "Okay, that didn't work. We'll need to do our regular investigative work. I'll drop you off at the house and we'll get together tonight so we can put the kids down and then we'll start doing our research."

"It sounds like a deal."

∽

At six, it was finally time for dinner, and William had knocked himself out straightening up his place. Even his bedroom, not that Vanessa would end up with him there, but he wanted to make sure he didn't leave anything to chance. He glanced at his walls and the prints of beautiful oil paintings of dinosaurs hanging in the living room. He'd thought if he ever found a she-cat to be his mate, he would probably have to take them down and put them in his office.

When Vanessa arrived, she was wearing a rust-colored sweater, brown slacks, and boots, looking like fall and just as pretty as could be. He took her light suede jacket and laid it on the back of the couch. "I hope you enjoy the steaks."

"Any cougar would." She smiled.

When it came to meat, he was all for it, just like most cougars were, so he figured he couldn't go wrong with it.

"I was thinking, if it wasn't too late, we could run as cougars after dinner. I wasn't sure how you would feel with having to work tomorrow, so we could just decide after we eat."

"Yeah, sure. I would like that. I don't run much on my own. It's not that much fun," she said.

"Okay, good." He had only thought of it at the last minute. Getting to know each other as cougars and as humans was important. But for now, he was glad the misunderstanding they'd had between them was gone.

"So the veterinarian who was your friend, where is he practicing?" she asked, as William served up their meals and brought them inside to set on the table.

"Colorado Springs."

⁓

*V*anessa was about to take her seat and she felt her body heat uncomfortably. Not that she would know his friend in Colorado Springs, but what if William chanced to mention to the friend that he was dating Vanessa and the vet knew about her wedding failures? Both weddings had been in the paper and both cancellations too. When she really got to know someone well, she'd talk to him about it, but in the beginning? She thought there was no need to mention it.

She'd been very careful not to tell anyone in Yuma Town about it. She'd had to tell them she was from Colorado Springs so that they could approve her building a vet clinic here to serve the cougars of Yuma Town and to know that she was a fully qualified vet. Beyond that, nothing else was important.

"You're from there, aren't you?"

"Yes, but I probably don't know your friend."

William eyed her speculatively. She was giving herself away, big time.

"Matt Appleton?"

She shook her head. She didn't know him. *Thankfully*.

"I'm sure there are several animal clinics in Colorado Springs," William said, buttering his mashed potatoes.

"There are." She cut into her steak. The problem was William could smell her nervousness and wonder why mentioning his friend in Colorado Springs would have brought it on. "So where did you have in mind to run?" She figured switching the topic to show she was interested in doing more with William would work like a charm to make him forget about Colorado Springs and that she was from there.

"I thought we would go through the woods out back and just run as far as we thought we could and when we're done, we'll return."

"Okay, sounds good. We could run out at my place sometime, if you want." She didn't know why she said that. They had barely started dinner and she should wait to see how this went. But she did feel that she owed him for giving him the cold shoulder since she'd been here.

"Yeah, sure, I'd like that. What do you have out there? About twenty-five acres?"

"A hundred, so plenty of land to explore. Woods, a creek, some great rock-climbing features for mountain goats and cougars, and a tiny waterfall."

"A waterfall? You have a waterfall?"

She smiled, surprised he would be that interested in a waterfall. "Just a tiny one. It trickles down the rocks into the river in a steady stream. Sometimes, if we've had snow or heavy rains, it turns into a torrent. But most of the time it's just a fun little flow of water that's pleasing to hear."

"Man, Hal and Tracey have one near their ranch, so does Chase and Shannon near their resort. Now you have one?"

She laughed. "It's just a tiny one." She held up her thumb and finger to show how small the trickle was.

"I have definitely got to see this for myself."

"It's not that big a deal." Though it was one of the reasons she had bought the land to build her clinic and house on. She just hoped he wasn't building his expectations up, thinking it was like the waterfall near Hal's ranch. Now that one, people could actually go behind, and it was a lot of fun.

"How's your steak?" he asked.

"Oh, it's delicious! It's cooked to perfection. Thanks so much for having me over for dinner."

"You're so welcome. I'm just glad we could finally do it, once we cleared up the misunderstanding."

"*Please*, don't mention it."

William smiled. He always had the most disarming smile and she thought he looked both dashing and a little roguish at the same time. That could be her undoing.

"Were there any cougars in Colorado Springs?" William asked, making small talk.

"Yeah, a few. But not like Yuma Town. I love that it's cougar run." Again, she had to change the subject from talking about Colorado Springs. If she mentioned too much about the cougars there, she might slip up about the two guys she'd been engaged to.

"Same with where I was at in Twin Falls, Idaho. I dated a

little, but never met anyone who was really someone I wanted to spend more time with."

She smiled, knowing just where this was going. "Yeah, me too." Don't ask anything about who she had dated, please.

"Are you ready to run?"

"Yeah, I sure am." She helped him with the dishes and loaded them into the dishwasher.

"You can change in the guest room if you would like, down that way." He motioned to the hall leading away from the living room and kitchen.

"Okay, thanks. I'll be right out." Before she headed down the hallway, looking forward to getting some exercise after a long day at work, she noticed the beautiful landscape paintings featuring dinosaurs on the walls in the living room. She smiled. She had all the *Jurassic Park* movies, and she'd read all about dinosaurs when she was a kid. Of course, they were always learning new things about them and that changed some of the suppositions they had about them—like most of the dinosaurs of the Jurassic Era were probably covered with feathers, according to a Siberian find and study. Dinosaurs had always fascinated her.

She wondered if pictures and toys and movies would depict them that way in the future.

She hurried out of her clothes and shifted. Then as a golden-coated cougar, she loped down the hallway and found William waiting for her in the living room. He was tawnier colored and she thought that fur was pretty too. She nuzzled his face in greeting, and then he led her through the cougar door in the dining room.

He ran with her through the woods out back of the townhouse, and she really enjoyed running with him. She wanted to do this again.

They finally reached a place where they could climb rocks, startling a couple of goats. She heard owls hooting off in the distance, one calling to another. Then, sitting atop the mountain of rocks, Vanessa and William looked up at the stars in the heaven and the full moon all aglow. A couple of miles away, they saw a sprinkling of city lights in Yuma Town. Up here, with the mountains in the distance, her place, and Hal's ranch even further out, she felt they were on top of the world.

Then they saw a bat fly overhead and she smiled. Perfect for Halloween. She realized William didn't decorate for Halloween. Was he even going to the Halloween party? He might not be into that sort of thing.

Then she yawned and he licked her cheek with his sandpaper tongue and she licked him back. It was time to head back to his place so she could return home to her own Halloween black cat and get some sleep before another workday.

CHAPTER 4

Once they reached William's townhouse, shifted, and dressed, Vanessa told William how much she had enjoyed dinner and the cougar run. "Did you want to have dinner at my place sometime?"

"And I can see your waterfall? Sure. Would tomorrow night work for you?" William smiled, not letting the opportunity pass.

She chuckled. "Yeah, sure."

He hoped he wasn't going too fast with her, but he had some catching up to do. And he didn't see any reason to wait and get to know her more slowly. What if she finally began opening up to other bachelor males in the town, or those who lived out of town and who were related to town members or had friends here? What if one of them began dating Vanessa and then William lost his chance to get to know her?

At least she seemed like she was up for it. He walked her out to her car and he was thinking he needed to get a barbecue grill of his own—just in case she wanted another grilled outdoor meal. He had to give Leyton's grill back to him. William certainly couldn't expect Leyton to loan it to him every time he needed to cook outdoors.

"I had a great night," William said.

"Yeah, me too, William." She took his hand and seemed to be deciding what to do next. Then she pulled him into her arms and she kissed him.

He was trying to kiss her sweetly, as in them being on a first-date kiss, but it morphed into something more. He couldn't help himself. He'd been wanting to date her since he'd first met her. With the way she was kissing him back, it seemed she felt the same way about him. More the better.

He finally kissed her mouth lightly. "I'll see you tomorrow night then."

"See you then." She climbed into her car and drove off.

He felt like he'd made a real breakthrough in getting to know her better. It still didn't mean they were meant to be together long term, but this was the first time in years that he'd dated a woman he wanted to see a lot more of. Running with her as a cougar had been magical.

The next day, William couldn't wait to see Vanessa for dinner and a run that night and called her that morning. "Hey, tell me if I'm bothering you too much, but we both need lunch and if you want me to grab something and we can eat at your place, I will."

"If you don't mind, you can bring me steak fajitas from Jose's Mexican Restaurant."

William hadn't expected her to agree so quickly and he thought that was a good sign. "That's my favorite too. What time would you like to eat?"

"Eleven-thirty, if that works for you. We shut down for an hour to give everyone time to eat. And then we're open at 12:30 for clients who need to come in during their lunch hour."

"Okay, I'll be there at 11:30." He needed to clear it with Kate, but he figured she would be happy to cover for him if someone walked in with a medical complaint.

Then Vanessa had to go and so did William to see their respective patients. He felt he was walking on a cloud, but as soon as he was free and Kate was, he asked her, "Hey, is it all right if I take off at 11:30 for lunch?"

Kate smiled knowingly. "Is there someone special you want to see?"

He chuckled. "I don't kiss and tell."

"Ohmigod, you kissed her already?"

Their receptionist, April Hightower, said, "He kissed who?"

Marcus came to see Kate with a chart in hand. "Who's kissing who?"

The other nurses, Elsie Miller in her crowned frogs scrubs and Helen Kretchen, both came to see what was going on. The only ones not there were nurse Mandy Jones and their emergency call person, Becky Sorenson, but they would tell her about it before long.

Smiling, William called in his next patient.

∼

Vanessa couldn't have been more thrilled that William was having lunch with her. It was nice that they could actually carry their takeout to her house behind the clinic so that they could have their meal in private.

As soon as William arrived with a sack of fajitas and sopapillas, she was so ready for lunch. Her staff had all left except for Riley, who was checking out the situation, as if he were her big brother.

"I'll see you in an hour," Vanessa said.

Riley looked skeptically at her. "That would be a first."

True, she usually took a fifteen-minute break and ate lunch

while she worked on patient charts in her office. She wasn't one to waste time.

William smiled. "I'll make sure she takes a full lunch hour."

She chuckled. "Yeah, but the patients' charts still need to be done."

"How well I know."

She enjoyed that about William. He might not be a vet, but he had similar responsibilities and she could talk to him freely about medical issues, either her patients' or his.

Then she and William headed over to her house and he smiled at all her decorations like he was really enjoying seeing them.

"These are great. I love your dinosaur skeletons."

"I thought you might. I loved your dinosaur paintings. When I was girl, I read all about the dinosaurs, before it was really a thing to do. I was just fascinated with them."

"Me too. Hence the dinosaur paintings."

"We must be oddities. When everyone else is interested in cougar photos and paintings, here we are loving dinosaurs." She unlocked the door to her home and once they were inside, he locked it for her.

"Differences is what makes us, well, human, at least half so. I have a human skeleton that I usually put out, I but didn't get around to it this year."

"Since you didn't decorate for Halloween, I wasn't sure you were into all that."

"I am. I love what you've done with yours. Speaking of Halloween, will you go with me to the Halloween party?"

She was surprised he asked her. He sure was moving right along. In a way, she liked it. There was nothing worse than a guy who couldn't decide if she was fun to be with or not. She'd had enough men in her life like that too. But in a way, she worried he was going a little too fast and they would end up in the same boat as she'd been in before.

"I wasn't sure if I was going to the party. You know, after a long day at the clinic, I like to just relax and be myself." She went into the kitchen to get glasses of water to go with their meal.

"Oh, you've got to. You'll have a great time, as evidenced by all the decorations here and at the animal clinic. I see you have a bunch of movies appropriate for Halloween: *Hocus Pocus, Stardust, The Witches of Eastwick, Practical Magic*. You'll have fun seeing the Halloween food and costumes. I had a great time last year."

She brought in their glasses of water. "I always watch one of those movies for Halloween." She set silverware on the table. "They have dancing at the party." If she was going to go with him, she wanted to dance with her date.

"Yep. And I'll be your dance partner."

She arched a brow. "You know how to dance?" For some reason, she didn't take him as the kind of person who would be into dancing, which really wasn't fair to William. She was probably projecting on him because her former grooms hated to dance.

She knew William was friendly to everyone, but she hadn't heard he'd dated anyone while he was living here either. Though she'd heard rumors he might be dating someone out of town, like at the medical conferences he went to so that he would keep up his credentials.

"I sure do."

She sighed. "All right. I was going to watch *Hocus Pocus* Halloween night."

"We can watch it afterward."

They sat down to eat their fajitas.

She laughed. "You have everything planned out, don't you?" She added sour cream, shredded cheese, and guacamole to her fajita and took a bite.

"Not everything. I'm in uncharted waters here and playing things by ear. How are your fajitas?"

"Delicious! Much better than the tuna fish sandwich I was going to have. And the company is fun."

"I feel the same way. So what are you going to wear to the party?"

"I think I'll be a…a female pirate in charge of her own sailing ship and crew. What about you?" She ate some more of her fajitas. These were really good.

She was thinking a pirate costume would be easy. She had a peasant skirt, blouse, and boots she could wear. She just needed a belt and a scabbard and sword.

"I'm not sure. I'll have to see what I can scrounge up."

"You mean you don't have a closet full of costumes?" She lifted her second fajita to her lips.

He laughed. "I've missed several of the Halloween parties because I've been out of town at medical conferences, so this one will be special. I have to give it some thought. I didn't expect to have a date for the night."

"Well, you can swab my decks any time."

He smiled in a way that said he was seeing a lot more into what she was saying than she had intended.

She felt her face warm, realizing he had taken it in a sexual way.

"I think I'll have to be a pirate on your ship, swabbing your decks, or anything else you need me to do." He made up his third fajita.

"Yes! Pirates it is."

He smiled. "We're going to have fun."

"We will." Well, she hadn't expected to become a pirate for Halloween and have a date for the Halloween party while she was having lunch with William. She liked that he really wanted to see her further. She was enjoying her time with him.

"What exciting things have you done today so far?" he asked.

That was a first for her too. Normally, the guys she dated

didn't care one whit about what she had to do during her workday. Maybe it was because William was in medicine also.

"I delivered a cougar who was having her twins in her cougar form. She wasn't from here, but her water broke and she couldn't make it home in time. But it worked out well because she didn't have a cougar doctor back home to deliver her."

"Well that's easier."

She frowned at him as she brought them cups of coffee.

"I mean that it's easier for the momma to deliver multiple babies that way." He smiled at her.

"Right."

He smiled again in his perfectly charming way.

"What did you do that was exciting today?" she asked him. She really was interested.

"I delivered a woman's baby, just one though. She was human and on her way to Loveland. She said her doctor had advised her not to travel this late in her pregnancy, but she had to visit a dying aunt before it was too late, and then the woman went into labor on the way home. It's getting close to Halloween, you know."

"Oh, wow. And yeah, I agree. I have more cases like that during Halloween than any other time of year. Is she still at the clinic?" Vanessa asked. They normally didn't keep humans at the clinic for very long if they ended up there. Every once in a while a cougar would come in with a bad injury and be so out of it, he or she would shift unexpectedly, so they really tried to keep it as a clinic just for shifters as much as possible.

"No. They transported her to the hospital in Loveland, where her husband and parents are meeting her. It all worked out well. The baby was full-term and healthy."

"So were the shifter babies."

"That's good."

"I agree. I love lunch, by the way. Thanks so much for bringing it."

"You're welcome. I thought it could be fun."

"It was really nice," she said, and was thinking she could get used to this. "I'm going to start our pot roast in the slow cooker, and it will be done by the time we're ready to have dinner."

"That sounds great. What can I do to help?"

"Can you peel the carrots or potatoes?" She hadn't expected him to offer to help her since he'd made the dinner last night without her help and he'd bought their lunch.

"I can do both."

"Okay, great." She brought out the potatoes, carrots, and onions, pot roast, and the seasoning package she loved. She set out a cutting board and peeler for him and brought out the slow cooker. Then she set out another cutting board and a knife and worked on the onions, then threw them in the cooker with the roast, some water, and the seasoning mix.

He finished peeling the carrots and she cut them up. Once he was done with the potatoes, she cut them up too and added them to the pot, covered it, and put it on high.

"That's a good way to cook a meal while you're working," he said.

"Yeah, I use it for brisket, corned beef, tough roasts, stew, lots of stuff. And then I can freeze a good portion of the rest of it for later."

"I need to get one of those."

They talked some more about cases they each had and then, unfortunately, it was time for them both to return to work. William had to leave a few minutes early to drive back into Yuma Town to the clinic.

He walked her to the animal clinic and then they said goodbye and he drove off to the medical clinic.

"Well, how was lunch?" Riley asked, grabbing a soda.

"Good. Yours?"

"I didn't have a date, so I imagine not as good as yours."

She smiled. "There's nothing to it."

"Are you going to the Halloween party?"

"Yeah. You?" She began working on her patient charts.

"Yeah. Is William taking you?"

She looked up from the patient's record and smiled. "Yeah. Are *you* going with someone?"

"I was going to take you." He began cleaning an exam room.

No way had he planned to ask her. That was one thing she had learned about Riley was that he loved to tease her. And she'd heard him telling their receptionist that he would like to ask her to go to the Halloween party, but she had said she already had a date. That was a week ago. Why hadn't he asked Vanessa in all that time? He was just too funny.

"How did lunch go?" Pamela Lang asked as she returned from lunch and moved around the counter to work on billing. She was their receptionist and billing clerk. She was a pretty dark-haired woman who wasn't interested in Riley, like Vanessa hadn't been interested in William. At least at the time.

Who knew though? Pamela might change her mind about Riley too.

Missy Longmire arrived and she was their other vet technician. Vanessa had heard Riley asking her out. And she had said no also. Poor guy.

"So, how was lunch?" Pamela asked.

"Oh, it was great," Riley said.

"You know I was asking Doc."

Riley sighed. "Yeah, I know, but she might not want to talk about her love life."

Vanessa laughed. She hadn't had this much interest in what was going on in her life since she moved here. Everyone was too funny.

As soon as William returned to work, Kate was giving him smiles every time she chanced to run into him. So did their receptionist and all the nurses. William was getting a kick of it. He was thrilled Vanessa wanted to go with him to the Halloween party. He would show her he knew how to dance.

The day seemed to fly by faster than he thought possible and he was ready to have dinner with Vanessa, barely saying good night to the rest of the staff at the clinic, amusing them to pieces. He heard them all laughing about it as he got into his car, smiled, then drove off to meet with Vanessa for dinner. He swore he could smell the roast already, and the delectable scent of the she-cat most of all.

CHAPTER 5

That night, William arrived at Vanessa's house and he loved that she had orange and black lights illuminating the windows. He hadn't expected that. She was fun and she made him want to do some decorating himself, if it hadn't been so late to do it.

As soon as she let him inside, she smiled. "Food's ready."

"Man, it smells good." He pulled her in for a kiss, having wanted to do that all day. "Thanks for dinner."

"Hmm," she said, getting into the kiss, acting as though she felt the same about missing him. "It was my turn to feed you."

"And we'll run to the waterfall after this?"

"Oh, sure. But it's not a really big one," she reminded him and put the food out for them.

They were soon enjoying the pot roast, potatoes, and carrots. "This is so good," he said.

"Thanks. I'm glad you like it. It's one of my favorite dishes for fall."

"Yeah I agree. I like your lights too."

"They add just that little extra touch."

"Have you figured out your costume?" He'd finally kind of figured out what he thought he could wear.

"Oh, yeah, I have a long skirt, peasant blouse, boots and I need a cutlass sword. Or a flintlock pistol."

"Do you think you're going to run into trouble?"

"You never know."

He smiled. He knew they were going to have fun.

After dinner, he cleaned up for them and she went into her bedroom to remove her clothes and shift. He stripped off his clothes in one of her spare rooms, then shifted and joined her in the living room. He knew her waterfall wouldn't be huge, but he loved the sound of water trickling.

They nuzzled each other, and then they went through her cougar door and she led the way this time, running through the woods and reaching a mountain of rocks. At the bottom, water trickled into a pond.

He loved it. It was just perfect for a cougar run. She bounded up the rocks and he went up right after her. Their own climbing rocks. Once they were on top, they snuggled with each other again, licking each other's muzzles and he couldn't be happier.

The moon was full and the stars bright. A star was shooting across the heavens and he made a wish. That he and Vanessa would continue to enjoy each other's company and that, if they were meant to be together, they would be.

After exploring and playing chase and tag for about an hour, they finally returned to her house and watched *Stardust*. That was a fun, feel-good movie. Watching it with Vanessa made it even better.

He finally said, "I'd better get going. I had a lovely night. Lunch tomorrow, if we can swing it?"

"Yeah, sure. Your place or mine?"

"Yours. We have more privacy here. And I like your waterfall, so tomorrow night, dinner here again? I can bring something?"

"I can warm up the pot roast or we could have roast beef hash then for dinner."

"Roast beef hash sounds good. What about lunch?"

"Pizza. Cheese and meat lovers."

"Okay, sounds good." Then he kissed her and she kissed him back, openmouthed and very receptive. He smelled her pheromones and they enticed him to take this further with her. But he knew he shouldn't push it too fast. Not unless she was ready. "Hey, I'll see you tomorrow."

"Yeah." She sighed and didn't release him right away. "I've had such a wonderful time with you. We could watch *Practical Magic* tomorrow night."

"It's a date." He kissed her again, and then he said goodnight and left, though he really wanted to spend the night.

~

"Okay, so we look into William's past next, right?" Addie asked Bridget as they gathered at Bridget's home that night.

Bridget put all four little ones down to sleep: Addie and Dan's twins—Mitch and Maddie—and Bridget and Travis's twins—Theo and Phoebe—all four of them born on the 4th of July. Talk about fireworks that night.

Addie was on her laptop, looking for clues about William's past.

Then Bridget was back on her computer, glad Addie's husband was out working too so they could do their research on William and Vanessa. "Yeah. I found pictures of the medical conference he attended, and he was the key speaker a couple of times. Here are pictures of William at a couple of the booths where the physicians picked up free stuff and here are some dinners they attended."

"There's a woman with him or nearby him every time he's in

a picture," Addie said, looking over Bridget's shoulder. "A blond."

"Like Vanessa." Bridget sighed. "What if William is still hung up on the other woman?"

"Do you have a name for her?" Addie found the pictures on her laptop and blew them up. "Wait, I do. Sandy Sherman. That's what her name tag says."

"She's a doctor like him. A family physician."

"But also a cougar?" Addie asked.

"That I don't know. I'll call him and see."

Addie frowned. "What? Wait. What happened to doing this in a clandestine way?"

"What if he's leading Vanessa on when he has this other woman on the string? You know some cats are wanderers and won't ever settle down." Bridget had known enough he-cats like that.

Addie let out her breath. "What do we have on Vanessa?" She flipped through some Google searches for Vanessa Vanderbilt, DVM, in Colorado Springs and had several hits. "Ohmigod."

"What?" Bridget glanced over at Addie's computer.

Addie shook her head. "She's been stood up at the altar twice. And both men were dark-haired like William."

Bridget joined her to see Addie's laptop screen. "Ohmigod is right. We need to get Kate clued in on all this right away."

∼

The next morning, Vanessa was feeling really good about things between her and William when she arrived at the clinic. It was a lot easier to like someone than hold a grudge.

She saw a bouquet of red roses sitting on the reception desk and smiled. "Who got the flowers?"

"You. We're all waiting to see who they're from," Pamela said, smelling the roses from behind the desk. "They are so fragrant."

"Who else would they be from other than Dr. Rugel?" Riley asked, as if it were a no-brainer.

Vanessa was surprised William would get her roses. It reminded her of Edward Givens, groom number two, who had stood her up.

She opened the card, not expecting it to be from Edward, of all people. She couldn't believe he would send them to her! If he thought he could send her flowers—at this late date after two years had gone by—to get in her good graces, he could think again.

She glanced at all the expectant faces: Riley's, Missy's, and Pamela's. No way did she want to tell them who the flowers were really from.

"They're pretty and fragrant. We'll leave them here on the counter," Vanessa said.

"Are you sure?" Pamela asked.

"Yep. They brighten the whole clinic." Vanessa was about to head into her office, but she caught the shared looks her office staff gave each other.

Everyone had sensed her tension and had to know something was up when she didn't smile after reading the card, but she wasn't going to pretend they were from William and she had no intention of telling anyone about Edward. Here she was feeling really good about her day first thing this morning, and now she felt a dark shadow had been cast over her whole mood.

She walked into her office and threw the card in her wastebasket with a small clunk. She couldn't imagine why Edward would send her flowers two years after he had left her. She hadn't wanted to know why, not after her father had made sure Edward was alive, drunk at his apartment, and had apparently gotten cold feet. She was just glad she hadn't made the mistake of actually marrying him.

He never had apologized, had never talked to her about it. It had just been over between the two of them.

So now after all this time he tracked her down to send her flowers and a note that said: *Sorry, Vanessa. I still love you. Edward.*

He was sorry all right and that he thought he still loved her was his problem, not hers. Though she suspected he really didn't love her. Maybe he'd had trouble finding another she-cat to date and he had realized Vanessa wasn't that bad as a prospective mate after all.

She had vowed she would never think about him again, which was easier said than done, especially around Halloween. She supposed that was why she had been reluctant to go to the Halloween party in Yuma Town. She had met Edward at a Halloween party and it eventually had almost led her to marriage.

"I don't think the roses are from Dr. Rugel," Pamela whispered to Vanessa's staff.

That was the trouble with their super-enhanced ability to hear. Vanessa heard!

~

William had several walk-in emergencies he had to handle, and he couldn't take off the time to see Vanessa for lunch like he had planned. He was glad she was fine with it, though he really had wanted to see her. When William was finally able to break away for an abbreviated lunch break, Riley called him. William couldn't imagine why. He was hoping nothing was wrong with Vanessa. While taking care of pets, a veterinarian always took the risk of getting bitten, so William did worry about that.

"Hey, Doc, I didn't want to bother you, but Dr. Vanderbilt received some roses this morning, and she seemed distressed. We checked her office and found the card that was sent with the flowers and some joker named Edward had sent them to her. I mean, the dozen roses. If you want to stay in the game, I just had to warn you, being that you're part of the family in Yuma Town and we don't take kindly to out-of-towners stealing our women. He had professed his love to her in the card, so it seems he knows her from somewhere before. The only promising thing about it was she didn't seem happy about receiving the flowers and wouldn't put them in her office. That could be a good sign—for you. Initially, we thought they *were* from you!"

William didn't know what to think. "I guess he didn't leave a last name since she knew him."

"Right. He just signed it love, Edward. I just wanted to give you a heads-up. She's been happier than I have seen her since she started dating you. She loves her job and she's usually happy at the office. It's just a different kind of happy, like walking-on-clouds happy since the two of you got together. When she received the roses, it was a totally different story. It's like she's now under a dark thundercloud, not smiling or joking with us like she usually does. So you need to cheer her up."

Hell, William wished he could have been with her for lunch today. "Okay, I'll call her."

"Don't, whatever you do, tell her we said anything to you about this. She didn't tell us what was going on. We had to surreptitiously dig through her wastepaper basket."

"I understand. Your secret's safe with me." As soon as they ended the call, William didn't know what to say to Vanessa, without bringing up the issue of flowers and Edward.

Then Kate walked into the staff breakroom of the clinic to have a late lunch also. She microwaved a dish of lasagna. "Do you know a Sandy Sherman?" she casually asked.

William's jaw dropped before he caught himself. How would Kate know about *her*?

"She's a family physician in a practice in Pensacola, Florida and a cougar like us. I've run into her at a few medical conferences. You know how it is when we smell one of our own kind when everyone else is human. Instant attraction and friendship."

Which didn't explain why Kate was asking him about Sandy. "Uh, yeah. I went to medical school with her and we even interned together in Twin Falls. But she ended up moving to Pensacola and joining a practice there."

"And you dated her." The microwave dinged and Kate took her lasagna out of the oven and set it on the table across from him.

"Sure. She was the only cougar I knew in Twin Falls. Why?" Sandy had nothing to do with William's relationship with Vanessa and if there were any misconceptions about him and Sandy, he wanted to nip that in the bud right away.

"I was sorting through some old conference photos and saw one of her and me and just wondered if you knew her. It's been some years ago, way before I met you and it dawned on me that she had said something about Twin Falls and I wondered if you'd known her."

"Ah, okay." He didn't buy it.

"So are you involved with her?"

William's frown faded and he smiled. "Okay, which of them put you up to it? Your mate?" Even if Leyton hadn't wanted to look into William's past love life, William knew he would do it for Kate.

"Pardon?" Kate would not be a good poker player. Her cheeks blushed a little and William knew the truth of it.

William shook his head. "Someone in the CSF learned I was seeing Sandy at the conferences. Maybe making sure I didn't upset Vanessa? I can assure you, I dated Sandy, but I love it here and I have no intention of moving to Pensacola or anywhere else. And Sandy and I do socialize at conferences, but there's not even any bed play. She's dating some guy who's a surgeon, and he can't get away to go with her to her conferences. So it's like meeting up with her and bringing each other up-to-date about what's going on in our lives. When I see her next time—and that's the only way I ever talk to her and only if we run into each other—I'm hoping I can tell her I'm seriously dating someone too. More than dating, if things work out between Vanessa and me."

"Okay, thanks for telling me. Addie and Bridget were worried the two of you—"

"Sandy and me?"

"No, Vanessa and you might need—well, they wanted to help. I don't know."

William sighed. "They should be more worried about some guy named Edward, who sent roses to Vanessa this morning, professing his love."

Kate's eyes rounded. "Edward Givens?"

William frowned. "You *know* him?"

"He never showed up for their wedding day, two years ago. It was all in the papers in Colorado Springs."

William closed his gaping mouth. "Addie and Bridget were checking on her too?"

"Well, yes. But he was the second one who did that to her."

"It happened to Vanessa twice?" William couldn't imagine anything so awful. She had to have felt terrible about it, and she certainly hadn't deserved to be treated so shabbily. She was better off without them.

"Yep, and no matter what, we don't want it to happen to her again."

"Okay, well, I was going to call her, but I wasn't sure what to say. If rumors are getting out that I'm seeing Sandy, I'll tell Vanessa it isn't so."

"Good idea." Kate finished her lunch and threw out her trash. "Everyone just has both your best interests at heart."

He chuckled. "Thanks. Riley was the one who called to tell me about the roses."

Smiling, Kate patted William on the back. "It will all work out if it's supposed to."

"I agree."

"Oh, and if you're looking to offer a home to a dog that needs one, Chase found a twelve-week-old Great Pyrenees by Lake Buchanan. Chase took him home, but he's got enough pets already. Of course the girls wanted to keep him. The puppy could really work in your favor. Chase said he's got everything for him to set you up: puppy food, bed, crate, dog dishes."

"Uh, Yeah, sure." Taking in a puppy would further endear him to Vanessa, wouldn't he?

"You'll need to take him in for shots."

"Okay, sure." Ironically, he'd never owned a pet. How hard could it be? "I'll give Chase a call and tell him I'll give Buddy a home."

Kate smiled. "Buddy. I like that name."

Once Kate left the breakroom, William called Vanessa. "Hey, sorry I couldn't get away to have lunch with you."

"Oh, no, don't worry about it. Some days are like that here too. We both know how it goes. But I've got to say something to you before someone else spills the beans."

He figured she was going to tell him about the roses and Edward. He didn't want her to feel she had to explain what was going on, but he did want to tell her about Sandy.

"I received some roses today—this morning. They're from my ex-fiancé. He was a no-show at my wedding two years ago."

"He must be crazy."

"That's not the worst of it. It happened to me the year before, another groom, another no-show. I had planned to tell you if we continued to date, but when the roses came, I knew I had to tell you before someone else did and you worried that I was seeing someone else."

"So there's no chance you'll ever get together with your ex again?"

"Are you kidding? No way. Edward never explained why he had done that, and I wouldn't be able to rely on him for anything after pulling that. I just felt if he got stressed, he would run and hide and get drunk again. Like if I had kids or something. So no. He's never worming his way into my life again."

"Good. I'm sorry that happened to you. I can't believe they would do that to you. I wanted to tell you something too. Kate approached me about a woman I used to date, a family physician like me, who was in medical school with me and we interned together in Twin Falls. I've met her at medical conferences, but she's engaged to be married now, and we're just friends. I wanted to tell you that because Addie and Bridget have been looking into my background as far as relationships go."

"And me?"

"Uh, yeah. Sorry. It appears we're both under the microscope."

To his surprise, Vanessa laughed. He hoped that meant she was all right with it. He was amused that Addie and Bridget wanted to make sure he was good for her, and he didn't hurt her too.

"They learned about my two almost marriages?"

"Yeah. They didn't want me to hurt you like the other guys did."

"Aww, how sweet. Okay thanks, William, for letting me know about your old girlfriend."

"I sure didn't want to have to start over with you all over again."

"No worries there. I've got a client I need to take care of."

"I've got to get back to work too. I can't wait until tonight."

"Me either."

Vanessa was just finishing up with work and was eager to have roast beef hash with William when she got a call from Edward. She couldn't believe he would think she would even consider being with him again.

"Hey, Vanessa, I'm sorry for what happened before. I guess I just wasn't ready to get married then."

"That's too bad. The roses are lovely, but too late. I'm seeing a cougar and he's really good for me."

"We—"

"There's no we, Edward. You forfeited our relationship when you didn't show up to our wedding. You know how humiliating that was? Not to mention the expense of the wedding was all on me?"

"I'll pay you back. I'm sorry. I was a fool."

"Yeah, you were. Do you know my father was afraid you'd been killed or something? And he found you were drunk at your place? Don't send me anything else. I don't want anything from you. It was over between us when you didn't show up at the wedding."

He hung up on her. She shook her head. Jerk. She hadn't thought she'd needed closure with him. But now she felt she did. He wouldn't have been the right man for her.

Then she smiled. Not like one hunky family physician seemed to be. And she was truly ready to move on.

She was surprised when William showed up for dinner that night and carried a white and fluffy Great Pyrenees puppy inside. He was so adorable. Well, both William and the pup were.

"Ohmigod, you are so cute." Vanessa took hold of the puppy.

"Who is this?" She hadn't thought William had a dog. She certainly hadn't seen any sign of a puppy at his home when she'd had dinner there, not to mention she hadn't smelled him in the house.

"Chase found him by the lake and I said I would take him in. I called him Buddy. I hoped it was okay to bring him over. I didn't want to leave him alone."

"I'm glad you brought him over, and he is adorable. Buddy is a great name. He'll need to be housebroken, if he hasn't been already though."

William looked clueless.

She smiled. "Come on, Buddy. Let's go potty." She and William walked him outside. She had a quarter acre of land that was fenced, but he was still so young, he just stayed near them. Once he'd relieved himself, they took him back inside.

After dinner, they put him in the crate William had brought and then she and William had a fun run to the waterfall. They finally returned home to take Buddy outside again for a potty break. Midnight wrapped her body around William's legs before he took Buddy home.

"You seem to be an animal magnet," Vanessa said, smiling.

"And kids gravitate toward me."

"It helps that you make funny balloon animals for them at summer socials." She had admired him to be able to do that. He'd been all smiles and having a blast as much as the kids were.

He crouched down to stroke Midnight's back and she purred while Buddy was trying to climb on William's lap. "My only problem is attracting the ladies."

Vanessa chuckled. "All the she-cats talk to you."

"Yeah, but that's as far as it goes."

"Why's that?" She really did want to know why he hadn't dated anyone in Yuma Town.

"I've always been really interested in this veterinarian, but she wouldn't have anything to do with me."

She smiled. "Sorry about that."

He rose to his feet and pulled her close. "I think we're remedying that now."

"We sure are." Then she kissed him, not waiting for him to do the deed. Kissing him was sweet ecstasy, and she felt like her own motor would begin purring with affection just like Midnight's any second now. But the rest of her? Hot, needy, and wanting. She vowed to take it slow with William, but her resolve was definitely faltering. Not just because he was sexy as all get out, but he was fun to be with and someone she could see in her life for the long run.

He seemed as reluctant to call it a night as much as she was, but they had to get up early for work tomorrow and it was already so late. Not to mention he still had to drive back home.

"See you tomorrow for lunch?" he asked.

"Yeah."

"I'll bring us hamburgers and fries."

"Okay." She kissed him goodbye then, and with his bundle of furry puppy, they walked out to his car. She waved goodbye to him as he backed out of her driveway, while Midnight stood next to her, watching too as if she missed the cougar and the puppy, despite how aloof Midnight had been with the bouncing Buddy.

Normally, Vanessa was perfectly happy to be alone at night after a day of handlings clients and pet patients, but she had to admit, she missed William's company too!

Later that night, Vanessa was sound asleep when she got a call from William and was afraid something was wrong with Buddy. She heard Buddy barking and whining in the background. She wanted to laugh but stifled the urge. Poor William was having to deal with new puppy parenthood.

"I can't get Buddy to stop barking." William sounded worried and exasperated at the same time.

"Puppies need downtime. Exercise him, potty him before he goes into his crate. You should put him in his crate periodically throughout the day so that he doesn't learn that the only time you're going to crate him is when you're leaving him home alone or going to bed. If you go back to the crate when he barks, it reinforces the behavior. Bark, get attention. Bark, get attention."

"Okay. Did that wrong all ready."

She smiled. "Cover the crate with a sheet to create a quiet, darker place for him to sleep so he can't see what's going on near him and during the day, a darker crate will help him sleep. Play calming music or white noise next to his crate. Reward him when he goes into his crate. Make it a game. Treat for bed."

William sighed.

"It might take a few days, but if you leave him alone, he'll finally figure out that he won't be rewarded by barking, or whining, or crying."

"Okay, sorry to disturb your sleep."

"No problem. It's just the fun with pet ownership. He'll get used to it."

They wished each other a good night and she smiled. She was glad William was training the puppy and that she didn't have to.

First thing the next morning, William was calling her again. She figured he was going to talk about dinner or something, but instead he said, "Hey, how do I keep Buddy from peeing on the floor? I take him out and he doesn't do anything, then I bring him inside and he puddles."

She chuckled. "After he drinks water, gets up from a nap or bedtime, eats, take him out. Watch him. When he starts sniffing for a good place to pee, he'll have his nose to the floor, grab him and take him outside."

"You are going to get so tired of me calling you about him."

She chuckled. "No, not at all. I get these questions a lot. All first-time pet owners go through the trials of puppyhood if they get a puppy and not an adult dog. You two will manage just fine. It can take some time though."

"Uhm, what about biting?"

She laughed. "Puppies need to learn what they can and can't do. It takes time to teach them to stop biting. They check out things with their mouths and teeth. So you need to have toys to keep him busy. When he's teething, he'll need something for his sore gums. When things are moving, they like to bite. So you're moving your hand and he bites. Litter mates and mother dog will teach your dog not to bite too hard. You have to teach him the same thing. Get beef bones and antlers. Don't get stuffed toys that they can pull apart. They can rip them apart and ingest them. Also, yelp, or tell them no, or uh-uh, in the same decisive way if they bite too hard."

"Okay, gotcha."

"If the puppy comes to bite you, always have a toy for him in hand and then give it to him when he tries to bite. I had a Lab that would chew my hands every time I came home from work. She was so excited to see me, that's how she responded. I finally began to teach her to get her toy. When I'd come home, she'd first run to see me. Then, as if a light bulb would go on, she'd race off for her toy, then return to me with it in her mouth, wagging her whole body to greet me."

He laughed.

"It worked. So I no longer had to carry a toy with me. She would get it on her own. If Buddy isn't getting the message, take him for a walk, put him down for a nap, do something else instead of playtime. Play gently with a tug toy, throw a ball, so you're not using your hands to play with him. Change out toys, so they're new and interesting."

"What about him chewing on my slippers?"

Smiling, she shook her head. "Watch him. Keep things up that you don't want him to chew on. Put him in his crate if you have to leave so he doesn't get bored and chew on stuff. Exercise him. If you sit on the floor with Buddy, that's like an invitation to play with him. When I would sit on the floor with my Lab, she would be all over me. It was like I was one of her litter mates then."

"Okay, done that."

"Exactly. We all do. You need to sit up on a chair or something so you're playing above Buddy. Don't take puppy on the couch or the bed. He needs to be housebroken first. As big as he's going to get, I'd keep him off the furniture, give him his own bed to lie down on, if he's not in the crate while you're there. And no feeding Buddy scraps while you're fixing meals or eating them. You don't want to feed him the wrong things or too much."

"Okay, thanks so much, Vanessa. You're a lifesaver. Can I bring him with me at dinnertime? I hate to crate him most of the day and then at night. When I have a break at work, I run home and take him out."

"Of course. We can take him for a walk too. Though that's another training issue—walking him on a leash."

"I need to bring him in for shots also. Maybe before lunch and then we'll have him at the house during lunch tomorrow?"

"Yeah, sure. We need to set up a chart for him and I'll give him an exam."

Then they finally ended the call so they could both get to work!

CHAPTER 6

For two weeks, Vanessa had fun helping poor William with Buddy, housebreaking him, teaching him not to bite, and not to bark, and not to chew on things that weren't his to chew on. In the meantime, the pup and Midnight were getting to be best friends. Watching William interact with Buddy and Midnight, and her, of course, Vanessa realized just how much she needed William in her life—permanently—24-7. The four of them were becoming a family already. They just needed to be together, one consolidated household for all of them.

She'd never decided something so quickly in her life, and yet no matter how many times she tried to tell herself it was too early for making a commitment to William, she wanted to in the worst way.

She was wearing her pirate costume for the Halloween party and William was getting ready at his place. Though Vanessa had told him she would just drive into town, there was no sense in him having to come out and pick her up and drive her in, but he was a romantic like that. He had told her he was taking her to the party and that this was another official date and she loved that about him.

He called her on Bluetooth on the way to her house. "Did you ever get your cutlass or flintlock to go with your costume?"

"No. I have you and you can fight all my battles."

He laughed.

"What are you laughing for? I'm serious." Then she said what she'd wanted to for days now. "When you drop me off at my place after the party, you should stay the night with me."

"All right. I would be glad to."

She smiled. She figured he would be.

"Hell, shit!"

The squeal of brakes caught her ear. She frowned. "What's wrong?"

"Something just ran in front of the car and I hit it. I heard a thud. It was a coyote, I think. I'm pulling over to check it out."

"Oh, William, be careful."

"I will be."

She practically held her breath when he was silent for way too long as she heard him shut his car door and walk on the pavement to where the injured animal must be. "William?"

"Hell, it's a wolf."

"How badly injured is he?"

"I think he's got a broken leg."

"Okay, I'm coming to help you. I'll bring my tranquilizer gun. Is he conscious?"

"He's breathing, his chest is rising and falling. I'm about ten minutes from your place."

"Okay, I'm on my way." She ended the call and rushed to get her tranquilizer gun and a large cage, gloves for both of them, and then jumped into the clinic's van and took off to meet up with William. She called him on Bluetooth. "Is he trying to move?"

"He wants to. His eyes are fluorescent in the headlights and he's lying on his side. He's tried to get up. A dog, well, wolf, can run on three legs if they want to get away from danger in a hurry, so I think he's had a bit of a concussion, or he would have been afraid enough of me to run off no matter how much his leg hurt."

"Okay."

"Are you okay doing this?" William asked. "You usually don't take care of wild animals, do you?"

"Sure. There's no one else available to take care of them."

When she finally arrived at the scene where William's car lights were shining in the night, she saw the large gray wolf and William talking to him. He waved at her when she got out of the van.

The wolf tried to get up just as she raised her gun to shoot it. The dart hit his hip and he yelped and then sank back onto the blacktop.

"I've got a crate for him. Let's get him into it and take him to the clinic." Vanessa headed for the van.

William assisted her in carrying the crate to the wolf and then wearing the gloves she'd brought with her, he carefully helped her move the wolf into the crate. She locked the crate door and they carried the crate to the vehicle.

"You look great in your costume, by the way. I think I might keep you on my crew a while longer." She quickly kissed him.

He pulled her into his arms and kissed her thoroughly, and she smiled at his eagerness. "I will ride the Seven Seas with you."

"Okay, but first, we need to take care of the wolf."

"Duty first."

"Of course." She drove the wolf back to her clinic, William following behind her. Then she was pulling into the clinic parking lot and William parked his car next to her vehicle.

He got out of his car and helped her to carry the crate into the clinic. "Do you need to call anyone in to help you?"

Once they set the crate down so she could take x-rays of the wolf's leg, she patted William's chest. "You can assist."

"I will do my best." Then he helped her with x-raying the

wolf and he looked over the results with her. "It's definitely a broken femur."

"Okay, I'm going to use a bone plate and a series of screws to stabilize the fracture. In a year, it will be healed up and I can remove it," she said.

"You're going to keep a wild wolf around for a year?"

"Whatever it takes to make him right. Sure."

They began prepping him for surgery when the wolf started to stir. He swung his head around and bit Vanessa's hand through her glove. "Ow." She was about to sedate him before he could bite her again when the wolf's form suddenly blurred in a blink of the eye and he shifted into a man. One second he was all furry, the next, he was a naked male, late twenties, dark hair, dark eyes narrowed at her. He wore some of her blood on his mouth.

"Ah, hell. I bit you clean through your glove, didn't I? I taste your blood in my mouth. It doesn't matter. You've both seen me shift. It's too late for—"

"We're cougar shifters, so there's no cause for alarm," she quickly said and just as quickly sedated him before he jumped off the table to try and turn William or kill them both and injured his leg worse. The wolf shifter should have figured she could stop him. But he might have been a little out of it still.

William was just staring at the guy. "A gray wolf shifter. I'll be damned. Okay, so we need to transport him to my clinic now and I'll take care of the broken leg now that he's a human."

"All right. And I'll assist. Let's get him into some spare scrubs. Riley always leaves a couple of pairs here that should fit the guy."

"Have you ever seen a wolf shifter before?" William asked.

"No, but I've heard they exist. Which we just confirmed." She helped William set his leg, then they dressed him.

They put him on a cart and rolled him out to William's car.

"We'll leave your car here and we'll drive to the clinic, patch him up, and drive over to the party. Marcus is the nurse on staff tonight who will watch over him."

They moved the wolf into his car, and then William and Vanessa climbed into the front seats.

"Okay, good."

"I never saw him coming. Suddenly, he was in the road and then I hit him. I feel terrible about it." William was at the wheel, driving them into Yuma Town.

"I wonder what he was even doing here," Vanessa said.

"At least when he comes to, we can ask him. And he'll heal faster than a normal wolf." William glanced at Vanessa. "How's your hand?"

"He barely broke the skin. We can take care of it at the clinic." She'd been so startled that the wolf had shifted and spoken to them, she had forgotten all about it. "I believe he thought he would have to terminate us for having seen him shift."

"Or turn us, depending if it would work well for him or not, if he belongs to a pack. Of course, he might have been thinking of getting rid of me and taking you for a mate." William raised a brow and smiled at her.

Vanessa smiled and rubbed William's back. "No chance at that. That's one thing that's good about us. We can't be turned into a different shifter species if one bites us. At least I don't think so. I've never been bitten by a wolf shifter before."

"I don't think it could happen either. Sorry for messing up our Halloween party night."

"You didn't mess up anything. These things happen and we'll take care of him. Just think, we'll have the story to beat all others tonight at the party."

William smiled at her. "Yeah, we sure will. I'm going to call Marcus to tell him we have incoming."

"All right."

William got on Bluetooth and said, "Hey, Marcus, I'm

bringing in a man with a broken femur. Prep the OR for me, will you?"

"Yeah, sure thing. Weren't you going to the party?"

"Yeah, we'll go in right after we take care of this."

"All right. See you soon?"

"Fifteen minutes, tops." Then William ended the call. "I keep feeling like we need to tell someone we're going to be late to the party or they'll worry about us."

"Or they'll think we got to fooling around." She smiled at William. "Why don't you call Kate."

William called her then and she said she'd let everyone know, though he didn't mention the man was a wolf. He was afraid everyone would show up to see a wolf shifter, though right now, he looked perfectly human.

When they reached the clinic, William and Marcus lifted the wolf shifter onto a stretcher and carried him inside.

"So what do we have here?" Marcus asked as they took the injured man into the operating room. Marcus was wearing his Black Panther costume that he'd worn all day.

William had hoped they would have a quiet night so Marcus could be at the Halloween party, but Halloween night was notorious for crazy stuff going on.

"The man is a wolf shifter with a fractured femur. Which means he'll heal faster than a human, for one thing and he'll be fine. There's no need to move him out of the clinic after surgery, since he's one of us, so to speak. But we'll need you to watch him overnight," William said.

"Yeah, no problem at all." Marcus glanced at William and Vanessa's costumes before they dressed in fresh scrubs. "So you're pirates."

"Yeah, I swab the decks. She's the captain." William motioned with his head to Vanessa.

Vanessa and Marcus laughed.

They took x-rays of the injured man's leg again, this time as a human since the one Vanessa had taken at her clinic was of a wolf's femur. Then William and Vanessa bumped heads looking the x-rays over and they smiled at each other.

"You know, I don't think we're going to have to do surgery. We can put him in a long leg splint instead. Normally the healing is complete anywhere from three to six months, but for a shifter, we can cut that healing time down by half," William said. "Even from the x-rays you took of him at your clinic, I can see some improvement."

"I agree. I hate to do something on a shifter that heals so fast when we could use a less aggressive procedure," Vanessa said. "And I'm sure he would feel the same. Besides, we should really have gotten his approval if we'd planned to do the surgery procedure on him."

"I agree."

"Who is he?" Marcus asked.

"We don't know yet. When he wakes up under your watch, learn what his name is, where he's from, and why he was running out near Dr. Vanderbilt's property as a wolf."

"Will do. Do you have any idea how he broke his leg?" Marcus asked.

William let out his breath. "I ran into him with my car. He raced across the road before I could stop."

"Ow. Okay. Will your car insurance take care of it?" Marcus asked.

William frowned at him. "What they won't know, won't hurt my pocketbook. I'll take care of the cost. No billing the patient. And we can keep him here, if he doesn't have anyone to take care of him wherever he's from. But we do need to learn if he's got family who could be expecting him and worried when he doesn't arrive home."

"Okay, that's what I really thought you would do, just asking."

Marcus smiled at him.

"And I need to take a look at Vanessa's hand after we're done here."

"He bit her?" Marcus asked, frowning and glancing at Vanessa's hands.

"He did, but just a light bite, as if he realized the danger he would be in if he bit me hard and was able to turn me. Though he did break the skin. Of course, we didn't know he was a shifter at the time, and he didn't know we were either. I was just getting ready to do surgery on him, he woke, bit me—I don't blame him there—and then shifted, which shocked us."

"Wow. That's one for the storybooks," Marcus said. "You'll have a tale to tell at the party."

"We sure will," she said.

They finished applying the cast, but before they could leave for the party, their sheriff, Dan, arrived to check on them to see what had happened. He was wearing a Batman costume.

"Is everything all right?" Dan asked, coming into the room to see the patient.

Their patient was still soundly sleeping, now in a hospital bed. Though he hadn't needed to be knocked out to apply a cast. However, for pain management, he would have needed something anyway, which could have had the same effect. But mainly, after he'd bitten her and he seemed so growly, she'd had to react quickly and keep him from injuring himself further or them.

"Wolf shifter," William said, his arms folded across his chest as he looked at the sleeping man. "We don't know who he is or why he was in our territory."

"Dr. Rugel hit him with his car," Marcus said, as if he had to make sure the sheriff knew that.

Smiling, Dan shook his head. "That's not exactly the way we welcome new shifters to town."

Dressed as Catwoman, Addie came into the clinic next. "Hey,

what happened?" She frowned at the dark-haired man in bed, sleeping like a baby.

"Come on, honey," Dan said, taking her hand. "William and Vanessa can explain what happened at the party. If we don't return now, everyone will be over here checking the wolf out."

Addie took in a deep breath. "A wolf? A wolf shifter? Oh, wow."

William gave Marcus a set of instructions. "Above all else, call me when the patient wakes." Then he checked over Vanessa's hand, but the bite mark was already fading. He applied antiseptic.

"I think it's going to be all right. I don't need a bandage. It doesn't go with my costume."

"Sure it could. In the last ship boarding, you were slightly injured."

She laughed, and then he drove Vanessa to the party, while Dan and Addie met them over there. Everything was decorated beautifully, with orange and purple lights, a wolf howling at the door—more of a scary one, not like the one sleeping it off in the clinic.

As soon as they entered the party, they were met with flashing disco lights, tables of food and drinks, a big dance floor, and cougars wearing every costume imaginable. They paused to check out a bunch of Yuma Town's residents' costumes. This was so much fun, especially since Vanessa and William were together this time.

Hal Haverton, the horse ranch owner and part-time deputy sheriff, was wearing a Clint Eastwood kind of outfit. His mate, Tracey, special agent with Fish and Wildlife, was Calamity Jane. Chase Buchanan, owner of the lake resort and part-time deputy was Captain America, and Shannon, his mate, Wonder Woman.

Travis and Bridget from CSF were Robin Hood and Lady Marian. Nina and her mate Stryker, both full-time deputy sheriffs, were Spiderman and Spider-Woman.

Deputy Sheriff Ricky Jones was a steampunk captain of a dirigible and nurse Mandy, his mate, was a steampunk detective. Ricky's brother, Kolby, who worked out at Hal's ranch, was Thor. The owner of the bakery in town, and retired CIA agent, Florence Fitzgerald, was a gypsy fortune teller and so was Ava Lamar, who worked at the bakery with her. Since Ava had psychic visions, just like her sister, Nina, it seemed appropriate. Ted Weekum, Hal's ranch hand, was Zorro. Kate was Dr. Quinn and her mate, Leyton, was a mountain man, Sully, from the same show. CSF special agent, Jack, and his mate, Dottie, were Superman and Superwoman.

And Vanessa's own vet tech, Riley, was the Joker. It suited him. Her other tech, Missy was Little Bo Peep with a stuffed lamb, and Pamela, her receptionist, Little Red Riding Hood.

Then everyone quieted down and waited to hear what William and Vanessa had to tell them and they revealed that they had a real werewolf at the clinic.

Everyone laughed. Only for Halloween.

∼

Then William was dancing with Vanessa and he couldn't have been prouder of her for the way she was ready to jump in and take care of the wild wolf, though he imagined some would have put the wolf down. It was a good thing they hadn't planned to put him to sleep permanently.

He couldn't believe he was actually dancing with Vanessa tonight at a cougar party instead of her standing off to the side, glowering at him like she was known to do at these functions in the past. She smelled of lilac and pumpkin, of she-cat, and sweet woman. They had danced to the fast-paced dancing and to the slower dances too, and all he could think of was that she wanted him to stay with her tonight. And how that would work out. He felt they'd been headed in this direction for days now, and he couldn't be gladder. He wouldn't mind the commute if he could just be with her. That's all he thought about when he left her at night, or she left his place. But he hadn't wanted to push things because of her previous engagements that had turned sour.

He couldn't be more thrilled that she was taking a chance with him. He would prove to her she could trust in him to be there for her through thick or thin. Everyone teased him about emailing her, texting her, or calling her every break he chanced to have at the clinic. Sometimes he went out to see her for lunch. When she had enough time, she would drive into town and see him for lunch.

Every night, they would get together for dinner. But he wanted to be there with her for morning wakeups and when they retired for the night. He realized he wanted to be with her for long-term, as her mate. He wasn't sure she would want to try for that again—at least not right away. But he didn't want to wait that long.

He was dancing close to her again, rubbing against her, smiling down at her, kissing her. "I don't want this to end between us." He whispered the words next to her ear.

She smiled up at him and wrapped her arms around his neck. "You're not getting rid of me for a long, long time. What do you think's going to happen tonight?"

He was thinking she meant a mating. He was afraid to ask and well, what the hell? "You want me to mate you? Please tell me that's what you want and I will be your humble servant."

She laughed and rubbed her body against his in a way that said yes! He was already hard with desperate need and ready to leave the party and return to her home right now. Or to his place. It was closer.

"Hmm, do you want to mate?" she asked, sliding her hands up his shirt.

"Hell, yeah. And we can end all this speculation."

"Yours?"

"Yeah, and everyone else's." He wanted to leave right this very minute. "I guess it would be noticeable if we left the party too early."

"We're both off tomorrow. It's the first time since we've been dating each other. I thought we would stay here and enjoy the party until the end, and then the rest of the night and day tomorrow are ours. It's time to do this, if you're game. Besides, I love Halloween and I met the two men I was engaged to at Halloween parties that eventually ended up in marriage proposals and disasters. I know you're really the one for me, and this time, I want to make the Halloween night truly memorable."

"I'm up for that."

"I know," she said, rubbing against his steel-hard erection.

"Just for you."

"I'm more than ready." She kissed him on the mouth, then tongued him.

"Are you sure we can't leave earlier?"

She laughed. "Not while we're having so much fun here."

That meant a lot more dancing, a quick trip to the table to eat some more Halloween-themed food: Mummy dogs, deviled eggs made to look like spiders with black olive strips for legs, ghoulie punch, vampire punch

And then it was back to dancing. He was enjoying the slow moves and the fast ones, knowing they were going to culminate the night with lovemaking.

He couldn't believe she had decided this was what she wanted so quickly. He figured he would have to date her for months before she felt she was ready for this. And he was surprised that she had met both of her ex-fiancés at Halloween parties. No wonder she hadn't been really enthusiastic about going to this one, until she began dating him.

CHAPTER 7

At the medical clinic, Marcus was reading a mystery thriller in the break room while the wolf shifter was sleeping when the nurse call button was pushed. The wolf was the only patient at the clinic tonight, so Marcus figured he'd woken up and maybe was in pain. He probably had a million questions for them as much as they had for him.

When Marcus reached the room, he saw the man sitting up on his bed, frowning.

"Do you need some more pain medication?"

"No. I need to know where I am."

"You're at the clinic in Yuma Town and suffered a broken femur."

"Where's the doctor?"

"He's at a Halloween party. I'm supposed to call him when you woke. What's your name?"

"Roger Heston. I want to see the doctor." Roger rubbed his head as if it was paining him.

Marcus had his phone out, but Roger interrupted him. "I'll meet him there."

"He might want you to stay here."

"You can take me. Just call him."

"All right." Marcus called Dr. Rugel and said, "Hey, he's awake. Roger Heston is the wolf's name and he wants to see you at the party." Marcus smiled and glanced at Roger. "He's been rubbing his head, but he doesn't want any more pain medication."

William said, "We can't keep him against his will. Just bring him here then."

"All right. I'll set him up with crutches and bring the wheelchair. I'll need someone to be here, though, in case we have a walk-in or emergency."

"Hold on for a sec. I need to talk to Mandy, since she is your backup." Then William was back on the line. "Okay, Mandy and Ricky are on their way. You can either bring him and they'll stay there, or you can stay there, and they'll bring him here. But Mandy says she hopes you'll come here so you can eat and have some fun too."

"Okay, thanks, I'll be there as soon as they arrive here."

"They're already on their way, be just a couple of minutes."

Marcus got Roger some crutches and a coat to wear over his scrubs, then helped him into a wheelchair.

"What's your name?" Roger asked Marcus.

"Marcus."

"The Black Panther."

Marcus smiled, but the wolf didn't. He looked a little woozy still.

"Tell me what the deal is here. That doctor and the female nurse—"

"Uh, Dr. Vanessa Vanderbilt is our veterinarian."

"I was an injured wolf and that's why a vet was taking care of me at first. Gotcha."

"And Dr. Rugel is a family physician."

"You're all cougar shifters? I mean, you smell like a cougar I fought one once as a wolf, but I remember the woman, veterinarian, saying they were cougars."

Marcus folded his arms. "You bit her."

Roger smiled a little. Marcus raised his brows. "You planned to turn her?"

"I had to do something to get her to quit sedating me."

Marcus chuckled. "I'm sure Dr. Rugel would have something to say about that."

"I take it they're together."

"You could say that. Not to mention the whole town is cougar-run so you could be on the wrong side of a bunch of us, if you'd done anything more."

"Point taken. Who's your pack leader?"

Marcus smiled. "No pack leader. We're independent, work together, play together, more like a family of cougars. Not like a wolf pack. What about you. Where are you from?"

"I'm a lone wolf. Looking to settle down with a mate."

"You're the first one we've seen around here." Then Marcus heard a car pull up. "That's my replacement. Come on. I'll wheel you out to the van."

"I can't believe the wolf is coming to the party. He can't be in very good shape to enjoy it," Vanessa told William when he explained what was going on.

"Yeah, he should stay at the clinic, but we can't really force him to stay there if he really wants to leave."

"I could have sedated him again." Vanessa smiled up at Marcus.

"That may be what he's afraid of."

Vanessa laughed, and then they saw the wolf, well, Roger,

being brought into the hall in a wheelchair. She was glad at least he had enough sense to allow that.

William shook his hand. "Sorry about hitting you with my car."

"Yeah, me too." Then Roger smiled boldly at Vanessa. "Sorry for biting you. I guess I should be glad you didn't put me out of my misery."

Vanessa shook her head. "I would have taken care of you."

"I thought I was going to be stuck with you for a mate."

She smiled and didn't believe that he felt he would be "stuck" with her the way the smile played on his lips. He was kind of a rogue. "It was a good thing you couldn't."

"You were fast with a needle."

She smiled again, but she didn't say anything about what he had planned to do to William. She suspected he wouldn't want to turn him in case he was competition for her affection. It was too late for that, even if he could have turned them both.

"What were you doing running as a wolf out here?" William asked.

"Full moon. I've been doing really well for the last few months during the full moon. I thought I was through with the shifting issues."

"It's too close to Halloween," Vanessa said.

Roger smiled at her.

"We found your car parked off the road some distance from Vanessa's home," Dan said. "We checked the registration and found it belonged to you, but no sign of you. Once Marcus told William what your name was, we realized you were the owner. We'll have the vehicle towed into town for safekeeping."

"Thanks."

"Where are you from?" Vanessa asked. "Can someone come and get you?"

"I'm from Montana. I had taken a trip to Texas to see a friend and then I was headed back when I had all this trouble."

"Would you like something to eat?" Addie asked. "I can get you a plate and something to drink, if you're feeling up to it."

"Yeah, sure. The food smells great."

"Do you have a pack member who could come and pick you up and take you home?" Dan asked, when he didn't answer Vanessa question about that.

"I've got a friend with a pack in Green Valley, Colorado. I'll see if he can help me out," Roger said.

"Any of us can put you up if you don't feel you need to stay overnight at the hospital for observation," Kate said. "You can stay with us. My house is right behind the clinic and since I'm a doctor, I can give you any help you might need in the middle of the night."

"Yeah, you know, I might need to do that. The trouble is if I suddenly have the urge to shift in the next day or so with a cast fit for a human leg, it's not going to be good. I hadn't thought of that."

None of them had.

"Okay, you stay with us and we'll deal with it if the time comes," Kate said.

"All right, once I'm through a couple of more days of the full moon, I should be good. I'll call my friend in the meantime and see if he can help me out."

"Good."

Vanessa heard William sigh audibly. So did several other people. She wasn't about to tell anyone what she and William planned to do tonight—not until after the fact.

Then Roger told them about how wolf shifters mated for life. Vanessa was impressed.

After Marcus wheeled Roger over to a table, Addie brought him a plate of food, some punch, and a bottle of water. Several cougars came over to talk with the wolf in their midst and William quickly led Vanessa back to the dance floor where they rocked to the music until the bewitching hour. After Kate assured them that she and Leyton would look after their wolf patient, William drove Vanessa back to his house.

That was one thing about having a cat. Midnight was self-sufficient, though Missy, Vanessa's other vet tech, offered to pick her up and take her home with her for as long as she needed.

So much for keeping what Vanessa and William planned for the night secret! Though Vanessa was glad Midnight would have company tonight too. She knew Missy would spoil her terribly, but she deserved it while the cougars were at play.

"You're so eager for this you don't want to go to my house?" Vanessa asked William, as they drove to his townhouse.

"Right. Unless you want more privacy at your place. I figured we could go there in the morning and spend the rest of the day there, just in case you have an emergency pet case to handle."

"That's why I love you, you know. You're always thinking about my patients too."

"You're at a disadvantage," he said, pulling into his driveway. "At least Kate can cover for me. You don't have anyone to help you out. Well, me, for now. Though I'm going to have to read up more about the subject matter."

She laughed, figuring he was pulling her leg. He couldn't really practice veterinarian medicine unless he had a license, but to assist her in an emergency? She suspected he could, and he would be a real help. No one would tell anyone at least in the cougar run community.

"So the question is," he said, as they left his car and headed for the door to the townhouse, "do you want me to move in with you now, or wait until after we're married?"

That was the thing about cougars. When they mated, they were mated, but not for life, like the wolves were. Even if the big cats married, they could change their minds about being together and divorce. They were more like humans in that regard.

"Oh, you're moving in with me. And we're getting married as soon as we have time off to plan for it and do it. Besides, I feel like we are a family already—between you and me and Midnight and Buddy."

He smiled down at her and shut the door to the garage. "That's just what I wanted to hear."

"Hey, it's for keeps."

He chuckled. "Good. I feel the same way about you." He took her hand and pulled her into the house, looking like he was ready for business and couldn't delay this any further.

She was glad because she didn't want to wait any longer either.

CHAPTER 8

First, Vanessa and William had to take care of Buddy. He wouldn't understand that she and William were on a mission to mate.

They took him for a long walk, and then returned home to put him to bed in his crate for what came next between the cougars.

In the bedroom, Vanessa pulled off the pirate's scarf on William's head and tossed it through the air. Then she began to slide up his pirate shirt, exposing his chest, kissing his abs as soon as she moved her mouth up his body. "Hot, hot, hot."

"You are too." He tugged off her peasant's blouse and ran his hands over her breasts and they felt so good on her silky, sheer bra. "Hmm, if I had known you were wearing something this sexy underneath your shirt, I would have brought you to my house sooner."

She smiled. "No way. I had to dance with you and end the night at midnight, perfect for Halloween. You are much too impatient."

His thumbs stroked her rigid nipples making her whole body tingle with need. His eyes were already darkened with lust, and when she ran her hand down the front of his trousers, she found the bulge there. He was ready for her, had been since they had been dancing close at the end of the party. No wonder he had wanted to end things early and come here with her.

She knew this was the right thing to do. Their chemistry mixed and matched and enticed them to want more.

He moved her bra cups down so he could caress her bare breasts with his hot hands. But then he reached around her back and unfastened her bra while she rubbed her body against him, eliciting a half growl, half groan from his lips. When he dropped her bra on the floor, she sat on the bed and began pulling off her boots, but he was right there, helping to take them off. Then he massaged her sock-covered feet and she leaned back on the bed and purred her pleasure. He pulled off her socks and then sat down on the bed.

She left the bed to help him remove his boots, laughing, when it was such a struggle to pull the first one off. "You know, the captain of the ship doesn't help the shipmate pull off his boots."

"I'll make it worth your while, Captain." He saluted her and she smiled, then pulled the other one free and tossed it.

She removed his socks and before he could leave the bed to remove her skirt and panties, she tackled him to the mattress and began kissing him all over again, sliding her body over his hard one, his erection a steel rod between them.

He grazed his hands over her breasts in front of him and smiled up at her. "Worth the wait."

She had wanted to wait to have sex with him because of the last two disastrous almost marriages. She had been afraid to commit again to a relationship. And she hadn't wanted to get too heavy into the business with him unless she intended for him to be her one and only because of the positions they were both in. She could imagine what her clients and his patients would say if they were bed hopping with each other, and then moved on to others without making any real commitment.

But with him, she found she couldn't delay the inevitable beyond this and didn't want to. He was the only one for her and she was glad her other fiancés hadn't worked out, that being with William was meant to be.

She kissed William eagerly on the mouth, their tongues exploring, their musky arousal turning them on even more.

She hadn't even thought of Thanksgiving or Christmas, or anything else other than just moving in together, and loving each other every spare moment they could share.

She knew she couldn't get away for a honeymoon any time soon, but they would have to carve out the time anytime they could. And that meant him coming home for lunches when he could and doing more of this. Talk about afternoon delight. She would be walking in the heavens with a quick picker-upper halfway through the day.

He ran his hands over her buttocks still covered in her long, pirate skirt.

Her love for him went deep. He was so attuned to her, knowing just how to make her feel needed and desirable, like she was the only person in the world who mattered to him. She was the center of his world, just as he was hers. She couldn't be happier to be kissing him back, rubbing her body against his, making his blood heat as he was firing hers up, and preparing for imminent penetration, a union she knew that would last forever.

She couldn't get enough of him and moved around to get hold of his belt and unfasten it. Then she was sliding his trousers down and tossing them on the floor.

He took charge of her skirt before she could remove his boxer briefs, his erection straining for release. He unfastened her skirt and slid it off her, then smiled at her sheer panties. It was a matching set. What could she say? She had bought it especially for tonight to get him all worked up. Though he really hadn't needed the sexy underwear for her to have that effect on him.

He rubbed between her legs, smiling as she spread them for him. Oh, she was so ready for him to penetrate her. "I like these panties too." His whispered breath tickled her cheek. Then he was kissing her again. But he was still running his hand between her legs, making her wet and needy for him.

She ran her hand over his erection, then began to slide her hand down his boxer briefs and squeezed his buttock, his flesh warm and his muscle flexing. He was a beautiful specimen of a cougar and she was glad she wasn't waiting to have him any longer.

Then he was pulling her panties off and she slid his boxer briefs off. He moved her so that her head was lying against the pillow, her blond hair light against the dark blue sheets. This was more like it, both of them naked, his gaze sweeping appreciatively over her. Her gaze raking his nakedness with as much intrigue.

Then he was kissing her again on the mouth, and she parted her lips for him, willing him to plunder her. Heat radiated from their bodies, their hearts pounding furiously. He reached between her legs and found the dewy spot that begged for his touch. She already ached for him with a desperate need that couldn't be quenched. Not until he began to stroke her and she was arching against his exquisite touch.

Hard, soft, fast and furious, slow and deliberate, every stroke raising the stakes higher. She had imagined this between them. Dreamed about it. But nothing she could envision was so real—the scent of him, their pheromones sending out signals that said this was right, they were meant to be together, the heat and feel of his muscles against her, the touch of his kisses—passionate and sweet, his lusty whispered words, and his admiring, lust-filled gaze. This was real.

She was running her hands over his hair when she tensed, her concentration on the impending climax. He watched her like a big cat, saw the end coming for her, smelled her tension, her happiness and joy, and he was ready to pounce, to cover her with his body, and push his arousal deep inside her.

She cried out with pleasure, the climax enveloping her in warmth and love. And then he was moving like a cat would, readying himself, pushing between her legs, allowing her to adjust to his size, and thrusting.

She wrapped her legs around him, glad for the intimacy between them and the oneness that made her feel more fulfilled. She couldn't be more thrilled they were doing this now.

He was kissing her, mesmerizing her with his powerful thrusts, his body gloriously rubbing against hers. This was a Halloween to remember. She would always want to be a pirate if her treasure was bringing home a pirate mate. She felt aglow as he continued to move into her, deeper, and she lifted her legs higher on his body so he could go even deeper still. It was also a way of saying he was hers, she was claiming her booty and he looked like he was all for it.

He slowed his thrusts and kissed her again, his mouth like velvet against her lips, hot velvet. His tongue found his way inside her mouth and he began tasting the sweet vampire punch on her lips and her tongue, just like she tasted his.

And then he was ramping up the thrusts as if he couldn't hold the climax back any longer. He tensed, held on, and began thrusting again, and shouted out her name in a way that said he loved her. He continued to press deep inside her until he was done, and he rolled off her and cradled her in his arms, kissing her soundly.

For the longest time, they just cuddled. Then he kissed her forehead and pulled the sheets and comforter over them. "I love you."

She smiled sleepily up at him. "I love you too."

She realized she hadn't brought a bag with her to use overnight! Not that she would need anything to sleep in. Still, she needed some other items. Maybe William had a spare toothbrush. When he had run into the wolf with his car and she had to drive out to help him crate the injured wolf, she had forgotten all about her bag.

And then her phone rang, and she groaned. She reached over to get it off the bedside table and saw the call was from Riley.

"Yeah, Riley?"

"I'm sorry, Dr. Vanderbilt, but we have a sick dog that was just brought in. Part Labrador and part Newfoundland dog. He ate a chicken bone and has been throwing it up."

"Tell the owner to feed the dog a slice of grain bread, or half a cup of brown rice, and then bring him in for an x-ray. I'll be there in a few minutes."

"See you then. And sorry."

"No problem. I'm just worried about the dog."

Then they ended the call and Vanessa hurried out of bed. William began throwing on his pirate costume. Vanessa had to wear hers. He went into the bathroom while she was pulling on her boots and returned with his shaving kit and from his closet, a small bag with a few articles of clothing.

"I'm ready to assist."

She smiled. "Well, hopefully, the dog will be fine, but I'm so glad we're mated—before that happened."

They picked up Buddy and his crate, dishes, and food and loaded them into the car too and dropped him off at the house. Once they arrived at the clinic, she took x-rays of the Lab-Newfoundland mix, and she found that the dog must have thrown everything up.

"He looks good. If he's still throwing up, won't eat, is lethargic, can't defecate, let me know. But it looks like he got rid of the bones." She was thinking she might have to do an endoscopy, rather than surgery, if she could catch it soon enough, but it looked like he had gotten rid of all of them, or had chewed the rest of the bones enough that they hadn't caused any trouble.

"Oh, I'm so glad. That gave me a real scare."

"We're glad it all worked out fine," Vanessa said.

Riley took care of the bill and when the man left, Riley said, "I'm off to bed."

"Us too."

Before Vanessa and William could leave out the back door of the clinic to walk to her house, Riley cleared his throat. "Are you—"

"Mated?" William asked. "You bet."

Riley shouted, "Yes!"

They laughed and headed home and Vanessa couldn't wait to move William over to her place the rest of the way—and for good.

Now, they had to discuss the wedding plans. No matter how much she loved him, and knew he wasn't like the other men in her life, the idea of making a lot of wedding plans made her believe she was cursed when actually trying to go through with a wedding.

She vowed it would be different this time.

CHAPTER 9

A month later, it was the big wedding day and Vanessa was feeling anxious about William being a no-show. Deep down, she knew he would be at Hal and Tracey's ranch for the wedding without fail.

Like her, William had a medical emergency call this morning to take care of. And Roger, the wolf, had returned to Yuma Town after having left the town two days after getting his cast on to stay with the wolf friend in Green Valley. Now he was here to have William remove his cast and was doing well and was grateful they had taken care of him after the injury and was on his way home.

William still hadn't put his townhouse up for sale either, though he'd moved in with Vanessa. She had tried not to say anything about it, but she kept feeling like that was his chance of last resort. While he still had the townhouse, if they called it quits, he would be able to move right back in.

Still, she figured the cougars of Yuma Town would chase him out of town if he even thought of not showing up for the wedding. He had made too many friends here and enjoyed working at the medical clinic so she didn't believe he would run off like her other fiancés. Still, it was just a case of the memories of the grooms at her previous weddings not showing up that was giving her chill bumps.

Now she had another emergency appointment, this one with a client whose dog had ripped open a package in her car and eaten a pound of chocolate and several lavender-scented soap bars while she was driving through Yuma Town on the way to visit family in Loveland. Suddenly, the owner realized her dog wasn't jumping at the windows to see the sights, pulled over, saw the wrappers, and about had a heart attack.

"She's always bad about getting into things, but I forgot all about the package of chocolates in the bags in the back seat. I never thought she'd eat soap too."

"Oh, I know. It's amazing what they will get into when you least expect it."

Hoping to have no other emergencies before Vanessa went to the ranch, she was busy giving the dog an emetic drug to make it vomit. Which it did, all over the room. The clinic smelled like perfume and mint—at least.

"She should be fine. Since you're going to Loveland, just be sure and check in to the animal clinic there if she becomes lethargic, won't eat or drink, and they can check her out."

"I'll clean up this and take care of the bill," Riley said, who was supposed to be at the wedding too. "You go. I can be late to your wedding. *You* can't."

She sighed. "Okay." But just as she was getting ready to head home and dress in her gown—because now there was no time to have the ladies help her to dress—a pickup truck tore into her parking lot, the driver slammed on his brakes, and cut the engine.

She texted William: I'll be there. I have another emergency. Sorry, honey.

She was too busy helping the man get in the door with the

golden retriever he was carrying to see if William was going to text her back, but she wasn't late. *Yet.*

"He got out of my truck at a pitstop and was hit by a car," the client said. "He wasn't hit hard, but I have to make sure he's going to be okay."

Another emergency. She took the dog in for an x-ray, and saw that the dog was good, no broken bones, thankfully. He could be sore and bruised, but good otherwise.

"He looks all right. I would have him checked over at your regular animal clinic if he stops eating, won't drink any water, or is lethargic. He doesn't have any broken bones, so you're good there."

The man looked so relieved and after having the exam, the dog was back on his feet and anxious to leave the vet clinic, pulling at his leash, no limping at all. The owner smiled. "You cheered him right up."

"An animal clinic will do that for some dogs. They'll realize they're feeling just fine." She smiled.

Once the client left with his dog, Vanessa grabbed her purse and said to Riley, "Okay, I'm—"

"Jinxed," Riley said, glancing out the window and seeing yet another patient.

"Who is it this time?" Vanessa had mornings like this. Evenings too. She swore around Halloween, and with the full moon out, it was just inevitable. Thanksgiving and Christmas too. With pooches poaching turkeys sitting out to defrost and packages of chocolate under the Christmas tree—yeah, she'd had a fair number of emergencies to deal with.

She tossed her purse back in her office and whipped her phone out to text William that she was yet delayed even further. At this rate, she would have to show up at the ranch sans her wedding gown, and just say "I do," and be ready for the next emergency.

"No one I know. Everyone we know is probably at Hal's ranch, excited about the wedding of the year—that's not happening."

Vanessa gave Riley a disgruntled look and he smiled and opened the door to a gray-haired woman carrying a box of meowing kittens. Riley hurried to take the box from her to help her out.

"I'm so sorry to be doing this to you, but I live way out in the country and some horrible person dropped off a box of kittens on our gravel drive. There was no momma cat. My husband and I looked all over. We are both deathly allergic to cats and I knew there was an animal clinic on the way to Yuma Town. I'll pay for you to check them over, give them shots, whatever, but I can't keep them." Her eyes had that glossed-over look when a person was allergic to cats. Her nose was red from wiping it and tears rolled down her cheeks.

"We'll take care of them." She took the box of kittens and Riley went to the reception counter and handled billing the woman so Vanessa could start looking over the kittens and get them out of the woman's breathing space. That was one thing the cougars didn't have. Allergies to pets.

As soon as the woman left, Riley joined Vanessa in the exam room and helped her check over the kittens.

Vanessa finished giving them their first shots and dewormed them. "They're about eight weeks old, so they're weaned. It's a good thing or you would be bottle-feeding them."

His brow arching, Riley glanced at her. "Me?"

She smiled. "It's my wedding night, you know."

"*If* you have your wedding."

Though she and William were already mated, so this was only a formality.

She sighed and got on her phone, knowing just who would

take the kittens in a heartbeat to foster them until they found homes for them. "Hey, Mae, I hate to be calling you on such short notice but—"

"You're supposed to be at Hal's ranch. What's wrong?" Mae Sorenson asked. She was known as the cat lady, for good reason.

"A woman just dropped off a box of kittens. They have their shots and have been dewormed."

"I'll be right over to pick them up. I was late to the wedding because I had to get Muffin out of the tree again."

Vanessa smiled. She swore the widow needed attention and was always calling the sheriff's department for a cat rescue, even though the cats could very well come down on their own if she put their favorite food out for them.

"Okay, thanks, Mae. We'll see you in a few minutes then."

Riley interrupted her. "I'll see Mrs. Sorenson in a few minutes. Go. To. Your. Wedding."

"All right. Riley will give them to you. I'm out of here." Vanessa heard cars rolling into the parking lot and she let out her breath in exasperation.

Riley glanced out the window with the box of kittens in hand and smiled.

"What now?" Vanessa asked, setting her purse back down in her office.

"Looks like someone is damned eager to marry you."

"What?" Vanessa went to the window and saw William getting out of his car looking dapper in his black tux, and all the others in the wedding party parking and climbing out of their vehicles. She wiped away tears. "Hold down the fort. I've got to run to the house and get dressed."

She found Shannon, Tracey, Dottie, Kate, Bridget, and Addie all getting out of a van at her house to help her dress. She gave them all hugs for being there for her.

"William figured he was going to have to help out at the vet clinic so you could have a free moment to marry him," Shannon said. "No way was he letting you get away."

Vanessa laughed, tears still streaking down her cheeks. She was going to be all red-eyed and sniffles if she didn't quit crying. But she loved him, and she loved her friends in Yuma Town who were all there for her.

Before long, she was standing next to the groom in her courtyard, overflowing with her wedding party and gathered friends, the flower bouquets set all about the otherwise bare garden, making it look magical as she and William were ready to say their vows. He looked like the happiest cougar in the world.

When Dan, who was officiating over the wedding, asked if there were any objections, Vanessa and William gave him a look that said that wasn't part of the ceremony they had agreed to!

"You have incoming!" Riley said.

Vanessa groaned. "Hurry up with the ceremony, Dan."

Dan sped through the rest of the ceremony and Vanessa and William said, "I do." And then William kissed her like there was never going to be another minute of peace for them.

She kissed him back, a little more urgently than she would have liked to, turned, and tossed her bouquet to Jessie, who was thrilled to catch it. "I've got to run," Vanessa said, kissing William quickly again, then hurried off in her wedding gown to see to the next patient.

"Enjoy the reception," William said to everyone. "We'll be there as soon as we can." He hurried after Vanessa, to her surprise. "I might not be able to help you with all that you can do here, but I'm not leaving until you can go with me to the reception."

She smiled. She knew he was the only one she should give her heart to. Already, he was proving in their first moments of marriage, he was just perfect for her.

William couldn't believe Vanessa had been stuck at the clinic for one emergency after another. At least for him, they had nurses and he had Dr. Kate to back him up if something came in at the medical clinic if they needed to take care of someone. But poor Vanessa was really stuck, and he wanted to do everything in his power to ensure she had someone as her backup too in the future.

After all the trouble she'd had in being stood up at the altar twice before, he couldn't help worry that she would do that to him—though he'd only had the thought for a fleeting moment—or two. In between seeing patients, Riley had texted William, telling him all the trouble they were having leaving the clinic. The last text he sent him said to just come and get it over with at the clinic or they would never get married today.

By then, William had already figured that out and he and everyone attending the wedding had carpooled to have the ceremony in the courtyard between the house and animal clinic. It seemed the perfect way to handle it anyway.

He loved Vanessa as she put on her lab coat and was checking over a sick puppy, Riley was helping her with whatever she needed, and William was on hand to assist her also.

Then the bridesmaids came into the clinic carrying bags of clothes so William and Vanessa could change out of their wedding clothes to take care of sick pets, then headed out to join their mates at Hal's ranch for the reception.

But then there was a lull—no more patients, and Riley told them to go. He would let Vanessa know if anything more happened and she promised to bring him all kinds of food from the party.

As if fleeing from danger, William packed Vanessa into his

car and they tore off for Hal's ranch. "Next priority for Yuma Town is finding another vet to provide care for pets when you need a break, because believe me, you're going to need some breaks."

She chuckled. "Promises you'd better keep."

EPILOGUE

Two months later, they still hadn't found a veterinarian who could work with Vanessa in a partnership, but everyone in the cougar community was on the look out for one. That was one nice thing about being such a tightknit community. Though the problem with being cougar shifters was that finding a vet who was also one was a trial and a half. They had just really lucked out when Vanessa had driven into Yuma Town and learned the town was full of cougars and they didn't have a vet and she wanted to set up practice here. Which meant William had *really* lucked out.

Vanessa and Dan had testified last week against the escaped convict for taking her hostage. He swore she had a pet cougar. They swore she was taking care of a friend's German shepherd and the man was confused. He swore he was allergic to cats, not dogs, and it had to be the cougar that he was allergic to. William and several cougars had attended the court case and had gotten a kick out of Dan and Vanessa's testimony.

William was getting a lot of grilling done too with his new grill—a wedding gift from several of their cougar friends—with promises he would grill for the whole bunch of them one of these days.

William had finally had time to clean out his townhouse and put it up for sale and sold it. His dinosaur paintings took center stage in the living room that was now Vanessa's and his home. She had warned him if he ever divorced her, she was keeping the paintings and Buddy! He loved her.

Buddy and Midnight had become the best of friends and when William and Vanessa were together cuddling while watching a movie on TV, the cat and dog would curl up together in the puppy's bed. If Buddy plagued Midnight too much to play with him, the cat would just jump up on the bookcases and peer down at him while Buddy played toss with his toys until he wore himself out.

At least Buddy was housebroken, but they were now decorating for Christmas and that presented new problems. Midnight swatted Christmas balls off the tree, and in collusion, Buddy chased after them. Vanessa and William had their hands full.

"You know," William said as he brought over cups of hot chocolate for Vanessa and him while they watched their first Christmas movie together, "we'll be able to handle kids by the time we figure out how to handle the cat and dog."

She brought over a large bowl of popcorn. "Believe me that will be a totally new experience for us and we'll be learning it all from scratch. But at least we have friends who can help us out."

"I agree with you there."

William and Vanessa started watching *A Christmas Story* and when they got to the part about the neighbor's dogs stealing their dinner. "Every time I see this part, I think of having to make a vet call to take care of the dogs that ate all those bones."

"I bet. I never even thought of that. I just thought about all that good food wasted on the dogs."

She laughed. She loved movie time with William and their nightly cougar runs. She'd thought she would never find a cougar she wanted to be with always. William was certainly that for her.

William cuddled with Vanessa after they were done with their cocoa and popcorn, enjoying the rest of the movie. At least they hadn't had any calls tonight.

Then Vanessa's phone rang. Scratch not being called in.

She answered the phone. "Okay, Missy, I'll be right in." She kissed William. "Hold down the fort while I'm gone?"

"No way. I'm coming with you."

And that's the way it was. When they were both off, if she had to take care of a client, he was there with her. Kate had teased him that he should get a veterinarian license too.

He loved Vanessa with all his heart and he couldn't even imagine a life where she wasn't the biggest part of it for him.

He put Buddy in his crate with a treat, and then he and Vanessa headed over to the clinic. Afterward, they would finish their movie, run as cougars, and end the night right, loving each other as mated cougars should.

ACKNOWLEDGMENTS

Thanks so much to Donna Fournier for catching all my name issues and reminding me of who needed to be included in the cougar town—we don't want to leave anyone out! And brainstorming when I need it!!!

ABOUT THE AUTHOR

USA Today bestselling author Terry Spear has written over sixty paranormal and medieval Highland romances. In 2008, Heart of the Wolf was named a Publishers Weekly Best Book of the Year. She has received a PNR Top Pick, a Best Book of the Month nomination by Long and Short Reviews, numerous Night Owl Romance Top Picks, and 2 Paranormal Excellence Awards for Romantic Literature (Finalist & Honorable Mention). In 2016, Billionaire in Wolf's Clothing was an RT Book Reviews Top Pick. A retired officer of the U.S. Army Reserves, Terry also creates award-winning teddy bears that have found homes all over the world, helps out with her granddaughter with a second grandchild on the way, and she is raising two havanese puppies. She lives in Spring, Texas.

ALSO BY TERRY SPEAR

Heart of the Cougar Series:

Cougar's Mate, Book 1

Call of the Cougar, Book 2

Taming the Wild Cougar, Book 3

Covert Cougar Christmas (Novella)

Double Cougar Trouble, Book 4

Cougar Undercover, Book 5

Cougar Magic, Book 6

Cougar Halloween Mischief (Novella)

Falling for the Cougar, Book 7

Catch the Cougar (A Halloween Novella)

Heart of the Bear Series

Loving the White Bear, Book 1

Claiming the White Bear, Book 2

The Highlanders Series: Winning the Highlander's Heart, The Accidental Highland Hero, Highland Rake, Taming the Wild Highlander, The Highlander, Her Highland Hero, The Viking's Highland Lass, His Wild Highland Lass (novella), Vexing the Highlander (novella), My Highlander

Other historical romances: Lady Caroline & the Egotistical Earl, A

Ghost of a Chance at Love

~

Heart of the Wolf Series: Heart of the Wolf, Destiny of the Wolf, To Tempt the Wolf, Legend of the White Wolf, Seduced by the Wolf, Wolf Fever, Heart of the Highland Wolf, Dreaming of the Wolf, A SEAL in Wolf's Clothing, A Howl for a Highlander, A Highland Werewolf Wedding, A SEAL Wolf Christmas, Silence of the Wolf, Hero of a Highland Wolf, A Highland Wolf Christmas, A SEAL Wolf Hunting; A Silver Wolf Christmas, A SEAL Wolf in Too Deep, Alpha Wolf Need Not Apply, Billionaire in Wolf's Clothing, Between a Rock and a Hard Place, SEAL Wolf Undercover, Dreaming of a White Wolf Christmas, Flight of the White Wolf, All's Fair in Love and Wolf, A Billionaire Wolf for Christmas, SEAL Wolf Surrender (2019), Silver Town Wolf: Home for the Holidays (2019), Wolff Brothers: You Had Me at Wolf, Night of the Billionaire Wolf, Joy to the Wolves (Red Wolf), The Wolf Wore Plaid, Best of Both Wolves

SEAL Wolves: To Tempt the Wolf, A SEAL in Wolf's Clothing, A SEAL Wolf Christmas, A SEAL Wolf Hunting, A SEAL Wolf in Too Deep, SEAL Wolf Undercover, SEAL Wolf Surrender (2019)

Silver Bros Wolves: Destiny of the Wolf, Wolf Fever, Dreaming of the Wolf, Silence of the Wolf, A Silver Wolf Christmas, Alpha Wolf Need Not Apply, Between a Rock and a Hard Place, All's Fair in Love and Wolf, Silver Town Wolf: Home for the Holidays (2019)

Wolff Brothers of Silver Town

Billionaire Wolves: Billionaire in Wolf's Clothing, A Billionaire Wolf for Christmas, Night of the Billionaire Wolf

Highland Wolves: Heart of the Highland Wolf, A Howl for a Highlander, A Highland Werewolf Wedding, Hero of a Highland Wolf, A Highland Wolf Christmas, Wolf Wore Plaid

Red Wolf Series: Seduced by the Wolf, Joy to the Wolves

Heart of the Jaguar Series: Savage Hunger, Jaguar Fever, Jaguar Hunt, Jaguar Pride, A Very Jaguar Christmas, You Had Me at Jaguar (2019)

Novella: The Witch and the Jaguar (2018)

∼

Romantic Suspense: Deadly Fortunes, In the Dead of the Night, Relative Danger, Bound by Danger

∼

Vampire romances: Killing the Bloodlust, Deadly Liaisons, Huntress for Hire, Forbidden Love

Vampire Novellas: Vampiric Calling, The Siren's Lure, Seducing the Huntress

∼

Other Romance: Exchanging Grooms, Marriage, Las Vegas Style

∼

Science Fiction Romance: Galaxy Warrior

Teen/Young Adult/Fantasy Books

The World of Fae:

The Dark Fae, Book 1

The Deadly Fae, Book 2

The Winged Fae, Book 3

The Ancient Fae, Book 4

Dragon Fae, Book 5
Hawk Fae, Book 6
Phantom Fae, Book 7
Golden Fae, Book 8
Falcon Fae, Book 9
Woodland Fae, Book 10

The World of Elf:
The Shadow Elf
Darkland Elf

Blood Moon Series:
Kiss of the Vampire
The Vampire…In My Dreams

Demon Guardian Series:
The Trouble with Demons
Demon Trouble, Too
Demon Hunter

Non-Series for Now:
Ghostly Liaisons
The Beast Within
Courtly Masquerade
Deidre's Secret

The Magic of Inherian:
The Scepter of Salvation
The Mage of Monrovia
Emerald Isle of Mists (TBA)